RUFFIAN

Emmy Ellis

Chapter One

"Look, why can't you just leave me alone?" Aster stared at the man in the car, a car he'd driven onto the pavement in order to stop her from going anywhere on her way home. She'd darted to the side so the front of it hadn't pinned her against the low wall behind her, and she should have run then, but something had compelled her to stay. To get an answer from him as to why he'd been nasty to her when she'd stood on Debbie's corner that time, calling her a fucking poof.

The man stared back. "Because I know who you are. *Albie*."

Dread piled in on her. If he knew Aster used to be Albie, then he knew she'd been born a male. He could know *Dad*. Oh God. Dad must have sent this bloke to find her. She should have known he wouldn't let her go, not when she knew so much. She'd told her father she'd keep her mouth shut, and she had so far. Why had he come for her now after so many years had passed? Why couldn't he just fuck off and leave her alone?

She didn't know what to do. Like she'd thought not long ago when she'd clocked the man was following her, she couldn't run to her nearby flat because then he'd know where she lived. But it hit her, with a solid thump, that he might *already* know. He could have tailed her home any number of afternoons when her shift on Debbie's corner had finished. He could have sat out here, night after night, watching.

Bloody hell, she should have left work at her usual time this afternoon, not stayed on until late to make extra money. At the time that had seemed an important thing to do, seeing as she had rent to pay and food shopping to get, but now, faced with this horrifying dilemma, cash was the least of her problems.

"I don't know who Albie is," she said, standing by her promise to herself to be *Aster*, never Albie in this new life she'd carved out. A new life she *deserved* after all she'd been through. "You've got me mixed up with someone else."

He smirked. "Oh, I don't think so. I've been watching you for a good couple of weeks. I'm one hundred percent certain you're my target."

Target? What did he mean by that?

"Seriously, you're barking up the wrong tree," she said and hoped she sounded bemused instead of afraid. She schooled her features to disguise her feelings.

"You've already admitted to me what you've got between your legs, that time when I asked for a bit of how's your father to see if you were the right target, so there's no backtracking on that now."

It was true, she always told punters what to expect. From past experience, it saved all kinds of hassle—and sometimes a punch or two—when they discovered she wasn't what they'd ordered, and besides, she felt it was only right that she be upfront and honest. Too many lies had been told in the past, and this was a new start. Except now she might have to make *another* new start to hide from this man. Shame, because she loved the East End, loved living on The Cardigan Estate. She'd finally found home.

But how would she escape again if he watched her? What if he didn't intend to let her go and got out of the car, manhandling her into the back? She'd have to get away from him. Run.

How was he so sure who she was, though? Her makeup changed her face completely, her long blonde hair extensions further disguising her. She'd had those done because wigs had itched. All right, it had set her back a pretty penny, but having proper extensions had been worth it. Dad hadn't seen her as Aster—that she knew of—so she reckoned she was safe to lie.

"So just because I've told you what I've got down below, you think I'm this Albie person? Who is he anyway?"

"You know damn well who he is. *You.*"

Aster slid her gaze down to the number plate, lit up by his headlights, and tried to imprint it in her mind. She didn't want to look at it for too long else he would notice, so she lifted her eyes a little to make out she was entranced by the bonnet, yet the numbers and letters were still in sight.

"Sorry, I don't," she said. "Never met an Albie in my life."

She walked away, chanting the number in her mind, trying to act casual, as if the horrible encounter hadn't happened and he didn't scare her. Her heart still hadn't regained its usual rhythm from where he'd driven onto the pavement at her, not to mention the fear that had flown through her when he'd revealed he knew who she was. Now he'd said he'd been following her, yet she hadn't noticed anyone doing that, nor had she spotted a car crawling along after her on her way to and from places. She was vigilant at all times, or so she'd thought. Had she let that vigilance slip? Got too comfortable now she was protected by The Brothers? The watcher in the alley opposite Debbie's corner would have reported anyone loitering, so the fella couldn't have parked in the street and observed for any length of time. He'd have been told to fuck off, his number plate checked, and if he returned, the twins would have one of their famous 'words'.

She laughed wryly. There she'd been, thinking her new hair and face, her clothes and shoes, even the way she walked and spoke, had erased all outward signs of Albie, yet this man knew who she'd once been. How? It couldn't just be her confession about having a penis.

She took her phone out and pulled up the notes app, tapping in the car's registration while at the same time remaining alert in case he got out and came after her—or worse, sped down the pavement in the car and knocked her over. She'd be powerless to get away then, and he could take her to Dad's, to the place she'd so eagerly run from.

She left her block of flats behind and continued on, putting her phone to her ear as though on a call. He might think she was ringing for help and bugger off. Surely he must know that all the girls on Debbie's corner were protected by the leaders of The Cardigan Estate. If he didn't, then he hadn't done his homework properly. That gave her a smidgen of hope. If he hadn't crossed all the T's and dotted the I's, he might not be that savvy.

At the end of the street, she looked ahead, then left and right to work out which route to take. Either side were residential homes, and while that was good, nearly all of the lights were off, and she'd have to run a fair way to reach a house with any on. Ahead, on the corner, stood The Baker's Dough pub, people loitering outside beneath the splash of outdoor lighting, chugging on cigarettes, the smoke seeming thicker tonight as they breathed it out because of the nip in the February air.

She crossed the road and sat at a bench table with two women. "Sorry for interrupting and coming off as a weirdo, but I just need to sit with you for a sec. Is that okay? A man's been following me."

"Bloody hell," the blonde one said. "I'm sick to death of not being able to walk around like men do. Really fucks me off."

Aster had known what it was like to be a man, although that was only in appearance, and she'd been young before she'd taken the plunge in becoming Aster. A kid, basically, nowhere near a man. Inside, she was all woman, but still, she understood the difference between walking in men's clothes as opposed to women's, makeup versus none. People *had* treated her differently, and she'd been less afraid as her Albie persona when out walking. Then again, that was a lie.

She'd been scared shitless, worrying whether Dad would find her, follow her. She'd been right to worry. He'd found her when she'd nipped out to do a bit of shopping. God, that seemed another lifetime ago.

"What's he want, the bloke?" The black-haired one sparked up a ciggie.

"Sex, most likely," Aster said, "seeing as that's what I do for a living." *May as well be honest.*

Blondie tutted. "He shouldn't be pestering you either way. Where is he?"

Surprised these two weren't openly judging her like so many did, Aster jerked her thumb back the way she'd come. "Down there. He's in a car. Look, this is going to sound odd, but can I give you his number plate, just in case?"

Blondie got her phone out. "Go on then, but how will we even know anything's happened to you? Assuming that's what you mean."

Aster hadn't thought of that. All she wanted to do was make someone aware of what was going on so if she was attacked or went missing and it appeared on the news, these two might see it and phone the police. She explained that to them.

Black Hair raised her eyebrows. "Blimey, you think he's that sort? If you do, then phone the police now or get hold of The Brothers. That should be the first thing that entered your head."

Blondie wafted a hand for Aster to get on with giving them the number plate. Aster recited it, then double-checked her notes app. Yes, she'd got it right, she just had to hope she'd *remembered* it right.

Blondie saved it in her own app and sighed. "Listen, we were just off to The Roxy, so if you want us to walk you to your place on the way…"

"I don't want to risk going there just yet." Aster glanced back to where the altercation had taken place. The bloke must have gone, because no headlights broke the darkness, although that didn't mean anything. He could have parked and be watching her through binoculars or something. The thought of that chilled her, and she couldn't suppress the shiver that attacked her spine. "I'll…I'll go and speak to my boss, she'll know what to do. She runs The Angel."

"Then we're sorted." Blondie stood and extricated herself from the bench seat. "Come on, then."

The three of them walked down Aster's street. Nervous, but feeling a lot better with company, she scanned the parked cars, checking all of the number plates.

"Someone didn't want their dinner." Blondie gestured to the full chip packet Aster had dropped in fright earlier. The end had ripped, and food had spilt onto the pavement.

"That was mine," Aster said. "He drove fast onto the pavement, and I... Fucking hell, I'm bloody starving. I really wanted that pie and chips." She didn't explain why that meal was so important, why having a *pie* with her chips meant something to her. She laughed to take the fear away, fear that had come belting back at recalling what had happened.

"That's shit, that is," Black Hair said, "when you're really hungry. Like the time I had nothing proper in and cobbled together this weird dinner. Pasta twirls, spaghetti, and I mixed it with a can of beans. I burnt the lot and ended up going to Mum's."

At least you've got a mother. Aster only had Dad, and he wasn't anyone to write home about, the bastard. In truth, she didn't really 'have' him anymore. She didn't *want* him either. "Good old mum." It was what was expected, wasn't it, that kind of response?

"She's a nice sort. By the way, what's your name?"

"Aster."

Black Hair tucked her arm in Aster's, like Tracy usually did, the woman Aster had made friends with on Debbie's corner.

"I'm Kallie, and she's Sarah. We can swap numbers if you like. Keep in touch. To be honest, it sounds like you need some mates. Do you?"

Aster shrugged as if what was on offer didn't matter, but it did. Friends meant acceptance. It meant you went to bed at night knowing someone had your back. "There's always room for more." She wasn't about to say the only true friend she had was Tracy and a couple of women from her former location.

They exchanged numbers, and Sarah tapped away at her phone, the screen glare lightening her pale hair. Aster's phone buzzed with the WhatsApp tinkle, so she checked.

"There, three-way chat," Sarah said. "If that bloke bothers you again, you can tell us about it. At least there'd be a record then if none of us delete the convo."

Tears pricked Aster's eyes. Two strangers—although not such strangers now—were prepared to step in and be friends, folks she could rely on, even though Aster was a… What? *You're a person.* She had to keep reminding herself that it didn't matter *what* sex she'd been born as, what her appearance suggested, she was someone worthy of other people's friendship. Difficult to do, considering her past, and it was an ongoing battle with her inner demons to keep slaying them, but…

"Thanks," she managed and typed where she lived into the chat. "I've given you my address because…"

"We know why." Kallie squeezed Aster's arm closer to her. "Us women need to stick together."

Aster had to be honest again. "But I'm not really—"

"Yes, you are." Kallie skirted around a lump of dog poo. "You're whatever you want to be, that's what my parents taught me."

"Then you're lucky." Aster wouldn't go further into that. She didn't want to sour this friendship before it had really begun. Offloading her past too soon, and all at once, would send these two scurrying off to find cover. *Been there, done that, got the T-shirt with* FUCK OFF, YOU FREAK *on it.*

12

Kallie and Sarah chatted about their jobs and life in general, and in no time, they stood outside The Roxy nightclub, tagging on to the end of the queue.

"I'll be all right from here." Aster indicated the watcher in the alley. "He's paid to make sure I'm okay. He minds the women on the corner, too."

"I wondered why a bloke stood there all the time," Sarah said. "It's not always the same one, is it. Is he something to do with The Brothers?"

Aster nodded. "And Debbie. Right, well, I'll leave you to it, and thanks for everything."

"Keep in contact every day." Kallie waggled a finger.

Grateful beyond words, Aster agreed, said her goodbyes, and turned, walking towards The Angel. She checked the street for cars, and only one sailed past, containing a regular punter at the corner. James someone or other.

She went down the driveway beside the pub, and the security light switched on. Aster climbed the steel steps that led to Debbie's flat, tiptoeing so her heels didn't make too much noise. She wasn't worried about contacting her boss. Debbie had said she was always available to discuss any concerns.

The front door didn't have any glass or a letterbox, but it did have a peephole. Aster knocked and glanced to her left at the car park. A couple of vehicles, some trees bordering the edge of the tarmac, and beyond, she just made out the back end of the cemetery.

A chain slid across inside, and the door opened. Debbie stared out, her face painted in a shade of worry. "What's happened?"

"I need… There's this man…"

"Get in, *now*." Debbie, no-nonsense, stepped to one side and ushered Aster indoors. "If you've been mistreated, there'll be hell to pay. What did he do, rape you?" She closed the door, putting the chain back on.

Aster shook her head. "No, it's just…"

Debbie shoved her hands on her hips. "We need the three C's. Coffee, cake, and a chat." She strutted off down the hallway, saying over her shoulder, "You're lucky you caught me in. I've only just got back from Moon's. I usually stay over, but something told me to come home tonight. Now I know why."

Aster followed her into a neat and tidy kitchen.

Debbie took a couple of Tassimo pods out and got on with making coffee. "Park your arse at the breakfast bar, unless you'd prefer to go into the living room."

"Here's fine." Aster sat, glad to be off her feet, her stomach rumbling.

"Sounds like you need more than cake," Debbie said.

"I bought pie and chips but ended up dropping it."

"I'll order us something from Uber Eats. What do you fancy?"

"Anything will do, ta. I stayed at work late and made extra money, so we'll go halves."

"Fuck off will we. My treat." Debbie brought Aster's coffee over. "Do you mind using my pyjamas?"

Aster frowned. "What?"

"You're staying the night. I've got a feeling it's going to be a long one, don't you?"

Chapter Two

*H*e sat in the cupboard under the stairs. Shoes and boots dug into his back, his outer thigh, but he didn't move. If he did, they might topple, create a noise, and he didn't want his father to know where he was. Six-year-old Albie was meant to be in bed, 'out of the fucking way, you little bastard', but he'd crept down to steal a slice of bread. He hadn't had any dinner, sent to bed without because Dad had said Albie being naughty at school and Dad getting a phone call about it wasn't funny. Albie didn't think it was, especially when he hadn't even been naughty. Someone had blamed stuff on him, the theft of colouring pencils, those pencils used to write bad things on the artwork decorating the display board on one side of the classroom. Things like piss and shit and fuck and Miss Waterstone is a fat cow.

There was no way Albie would do that, he'd never steal, and he wouldn't write mean words about Miss either. Miss was his favourite person, and she'd been so upset when Christopher Richmond had said Albie had done it. Hurt, like she'd thought she and Albie were friends, and now it seemed they weren't. But they were, at least from Albie's side of things, only he hadn't had any time to tell her, to make things better again. It was Friday an' all, and there was an inset day on Monday, so he'd have to wait until Tuesday to get things straight. That was a long time, and he'd spend all weekend getting tied in knots, working out what to say.

Christopher was a right pig, and he bullied everyone, so why couldn't Miss see through his lies? Albie wasn't bad at school, it was the only place he felt safe and happy, yet Miss had taken Christopher's side, all because he'd been crying, shoving his fists into his eyes the same as the characters did in cartoons, except no tears had squirted out like they did on the telly.

"I'll be ringing your mum," Miss had said to Albie.

Albie and his dad hadn't told the school Mum wasn't with them anymore. Albie had been sworn to secrecy, although why, he wasn't sure. Dad had said she'd gone to live somewhere else, she was too busy working to stay at their house, so why couldn't Albie tell anyone that? He missed her. At least he'd had someone to stick up for him when she'd been around. Even though Dad had given her a clout for it, she'd still tried to protect her son. Now, it was just him and Dad, the monster. Oh, and his friend who was a bully like Christopher.

"Please don't, Miss," Albie had said.

"Well, you can't go round calling people a fat cow, Albie, it isn't nice."

Dad had said Miss was fat when he'd gone to parents' evening that time. He reckoned she needed to go on a diet and stop eating cakes. Albie didn't see her that way. She was soft and squidgy and gave him a cuddle every morning when he walked into the cloakroom. She cuddled everyone.

"But I didn't!" Albie had scrunched his hands into fists. Would she stop being so nice to him now?

"Y-you d-did," Christopher had stuttered, great big sobs coming out of him.

They were made-up sobs, Albie knew it, but Miss didn't. She'd pulled Christopher to her side and hugged him. Christopher had smirked at Albie and pulled a mean face.

"He's just poked his tongue out at me," Albie had said.

Christopher had cried again, loudly. "I-I didn't! Miss, he's a liar."

"Now then, you two…" Miss had pointed to the back of the classroom. "Albie, go and sit in Reflection Corner and think about what you've done. Christopher, go back to your table, please."

Reflection Corner was where the naughty kids went, and it was Albie's first time to sit on the multicoloured beanbag and think about his actions — actions he hadn't even played out. It was unfair, sitting there with everyone staring at him, probably glad they weren't in his hole-in-the-sole shoes. Dad said there was life in them yet, and until his toes poked through the fronts, he had to wear them.

Albie hated everyone at the minute. Everything was so unfair.

In the darkness of the cupboard, he closed his eyes, hoping the memories would go away, and if it wasn't for the boots and whatnot poking at him, he'd almost think he was on that beanbag again. Except he wasn't, and right now, he had a more important worry to deal with. He hadn't been able to get upstairs quickly enough when the doorbell had rung. Dad had been in the living room, Albie in the kitchen trying not to let the bread bag rustle, and the ding-dong had scared the life out of him. Before Dad could see him, and frightened in case whoever was at the door came into the kitchen once they'd entered the house, spotting him being a thief, Albie had shot into the cupboard while Dad's back had been turned as he'd walked down the hallway to open the front door.

Now, he was too scared to move. Dad and his friend, Muttley, sounded as if they were in the living room, but if that door was open and one of them sat on the far end of the sofa, they'd see him creeping out to go upstairs. Ignoring Dad's orders in the first place to get the bread had been pushing it, so coming out of the cupboard in full view would mean a smack or worse.

The cupboard door wasn't quite shut, and a slither of light from the harsh hallway bulb pasted a line of light on the wall to Albie's right. He played shadow puppets with his hands for a while, creating a bunny, a love heart, and numerous other things until the

21

men's voices rose and he lowered his hands to his knees.

"It's time," Muttley said.

"I dunno. He's not quite there yet. Still got too many soft edges."

"Then toughen him up."

"I've tried, but there's something not right about him. He's a bit of a pansy if I'm being honest. He cries more often than not."

"Well, there's nothing like throwing him in at the deep end. He'll soon get that hard edge."

Someone sighed. Dad? And who were they talking about?

"Listen," Dad said, "we can't afford for him to fuck things up, and as it stands, he will. He's too much like her. Got a moral compass."

"Then we'll have a word, tell him how it's going to be. Give him the rules and explain what we expect of him. Also tell him what will happen if he fucks up."

Dad's horrible laugh belted out. "He'd shit himself."

"That's the point."

The pair shared a chuckle or two, and Albie had the urge to run, to be anywhere but here. He peeked out. No one stood in view in the living room. They were probably standing by Dad's drinks globe, an ugly thing that contained bottles of stuff that sent his father's breath all smelly.

Albie carefully got up, grateful none of the boots clonked. He clambered over them to the gap and checked the living room again. All clear. He pushed the door slowly, eased out, and closed it enough to leave the same gap as before, in case Dad noticed. A sidle along the hallway, and he was at the bottom of the stairs. None of them ever creaked, but still, he was careful going up, and let out a long breath at the top.

In his room, he huddled under the covers, his stomach rumbling. He couldn't wait for the morning to come. At least he'd get to have toast or cereal, then a sandwich for lunch, and on Saturday evenings, Dad always went to the chippy, the one highlight of Albie's week, where he'd get a handful of chips and a sausage, maybe some of Dad's mushy peas and gravy if he was lucky. Once, Dad had shared his can of Coke, and Albie had cried, overwhelmed by it. Dad had never shared his Coke before.

The thud of footsteps on the stairs had Albie's knees knocking, his teeth chattering, and he turned onto his side, away from the door, scrunching his eyes closed.

"You awake, kid?"

Albie remained as still as he could, but then his body shook. A rough shove to his shoulder, then Dad

23

gripped his arm and forced him onto his back. Albie pretended he'd just woken up—he'd done it many times in the past—and blinked, peering up at his father.

"It's time," Dad said, like Albie was meant to know what that meant. "Come on."

Dad dragged Albie out of bed and pushed him towards the top of the stairs where a suitcase stood, a big one. Burgundy with cream caps on the corners. Dad grabbed the handle and hefted the case downstairs, Albie following, his skin prickling with those weird little lumps that always came up when he was scared. At the bottom, Albie followed Dad into the living room. Suitcase dumped on the sofa, Dad opened it up. Albie glanced at Muttley who stared at him with those mean brown eyes of his, eyes that sat beneath a big forehead that stuck out like a shelf.

"Plenty big enough," Muttley said, "as you well know, Steve."

They sniggered.

"I'll leave it open a bit so he can breathe," Dad said. "Wouldn't want him suffocating."

"No, he's too valuable."

Albie didn't know what they were on about and stood beside the blank telly, fiddling with his fingers. He scrunched his toes into the carpet, and something

24

in the fluff stabbed into the underside of his big toe. Dad didn't hoover much.

"I'd better feed him," Dad said.

"I'll get him some chips on the way."

Albie could just do with chips. He didn't even need the sausage or the peas and gravy, just one long chip would do. His tummy let out a strange noise, and his mouth watered.

Dad turned to him. "Look, it's about time you earnt your keep. You're the right size for what we need, so you're going to do some jobs for us. Once we get to where we're going, I'll tell you what to do, but until then, put your coat and shoes on, then get in the suitcase."

Chapter Three

In the restaurant, one in the arse end of nowhere on the outskirts of The Tick-Tock Estate so his vulnerability at being seen with a woman wasn't clocked by anyone he knew, George Wilkes frowned at his dinner guest. The fat ginger eyebrows of his disguise pulled tight where he'd used extra-sticky stuff so they didn't fall off.

"Is this a date or a fucking therapy session, Janet?"

He couldn't work out this relationship lark. Janet had said therapy was free when you were a couple. Something about it being the done thing to talk about your problems and give advice to your other half, but he hadn't known that until she'd told him. It wasn't as if he'd had role model parents to show him what a proper romantic union was like, was it. Mum hadn't been able to talk to George's fake father, Richard, about anything unless he'd let her, and as for his real dad, Ronald Cardigan, there hadn't been much talking there except for Ron telling her what to do, what to say, how to act. George had nothing to base his expectations of a relationship on, not that side of it.

Previous to Janet, for a long while he'd only had his hand for company in the bedroom department, steering clear of women, the whole love thing, which he'd felt made life messy with its up and downs and rules. Greg, his twin, agreed that women fucked things up, so they'd gone along without them. Basically, George had been clueless, emotionally stunted when it came to anything serious with a bird. It had taken some getting used to, *sharing* his feelings for free with someone other than his brother, and he was confused as bollocks, because just now Janet had sounded suspiciously like she was slipping in a cheeky bit of *proper* therapy advice, the sort he used to pay her for. The sort that usually had him zoning out, only this time, she'd hit a nerve.

"Can't you just give it a go?" she asked. "One shot to the forehead, job done."

How amusing that she's basically condoning what I do, giving me advice on kills, when she normally spouts about having some ethic she has to stick to, where she'd have to inform the police if she knew I was about to commit murder.

Has our relationship changed her?

He studied her. She didn't bother doing those stupid eyes other women did, letting them go all soft and batting her lashes to get her own way. She wasn't that sort of tart. Straight to the point, was Janet, and sometimes it got right on his nellies because he saw himself far too often in her, a mirror reflecting how he behaved and how it was seen by others. Hard. Blunt. The difference was, she didn't have the equivalent of Mad George sitting on her shoulder, egging her on to do things no 'normal' person would do.

What the fuck's normal anyway? We're all one step away from insanity.

He used to struggle to contain that side of him. The one where a switch flicked in his head, then he went off on one, sometimes not even remembering what he'd done once he'd come out of the red mist and saw the results of his handiwork. In his former therapy sessions, Janet had helped him to cage the beast somewhat, but George hadn't felt right, like a chunk of him had been missing. He'd skipped some sessions with her, let Mad out in the warehouse, and then he'd felt whole again.

A while back, Greg had seemed to understand that Mad was as much a part of George as his heart was, that he needed Mad in order to stay alive. Greg had told him Mad needed an outlet, for George to get rid of Mad's urges once and for all, so they'd gone around like they had at the beginning of their criminal career, hunting bad people down. Mad had kneecapped a few, given others a Cheshire smile, some suffering both, just for shits and giggles. George had returned to his roots, to the days when they'd first started helping Ron out as bully boys aged fifteen, and it had felt good. Too good. Recently, that had stopped, the extracurricular activities. Greg reckoned since George had got a buildup of suppressed Mad out of his system—or so he thought—he could go back to letting him out only in the warehouse.

The problem was, George was getting bored. The same old routine. Search for the baddie, take them to the warehouse, hurt them for whatever amount of time until George let Mad out, kill them, then chop them up and dump them in the Thames. A pattern, tried and tested, true, but it was so...last week. The hunt wasn't as thrilling anymore, and neither were the warehouse sessions. They didn't hold the same appeal. He'd found himself allowing Mad to escalate, to think up worse and worse torture methods to keep his alter ego satisfied. He wanted more than that now, something extra, different, and here was Janet, trying to get him to give that up. Trying to mould him. What, into someone *she* wanted him to be? She'd known from the start who he was, what he did, and it seemed she was like many other women, trying to change him once she'd got her claws into him. Made him feel things for her he'd vowed never to feel for any woman.

Was she off her rocker? Didn't she know him *at all*? Didn't she realise if she turned to emotional coercion, he'd pull back and likely end things? Yeah, he cared about her enough to want to please her, but he wasn't going to be the real George if he cut Mad out. He wouldn't feel complete.

He leant forward and prepared to lower his voice so no earwiggers caught what he was about to say. "You want me to take people to the warehouse, question them 'politely', as you put it, then, when I've got all the information I need, just shoot them in the fucking forehead?" *How sodding lame.* "No cricket stump, no rack, no other tool on my table?" He laughed. "Next you'll be telling me not to tie them to the chair with rope, a tradition, as you well know."

She shrugged. "Would that be such a bad thing?"

"Are you having a giraffe?"

She folded her hands on the table, a knuckle resting against the side of her empty pudding bowl. Custard clung to the edge. "Listen, Mad defines you more than you want to admit. I've been watching you lately, and you turn into Mad at the drop of a hat sometimes, even when just with me. I see him in your eyes. You once told me you had to wait for him to burst out, like he's always inside you, lurking, that when it comes to…doing what you do, you have to build up to become him, but I don't believe that. The time between being George and Mad is shortening, like it did before you came for therapy in the first place, and I'm worried you're going to snap before you've had time to think things through. I'm frightened the red mist will come when you least expect it, then you'll get caught."

"Why would I get caught? I'd be in the fucking warehouse, safe, where Greg can step in if I go too far. He's always with me for the most part. If I'm not with him, I'm with you, and it looks like you've taken lessons from my brother because you're trying to get me to rein Mad in. Again. He's tried it more than I've had hot dinners, and it hasn't worked."

She sighed, like he was thick as pig shit. "You don't get it, do you?"

"Get what?"

"You *are* alone sometimes. Like when you drive to meet me—and when you leave to go home. What if Mad pays you a visit *then*? And what if you get no warning he's coming? What if it's not your conscious *choice* to let him in?"

He sat back, hiding a pinch of guilt that would tell her he'd lied to her in the past. He'd done some research about his 'condition' as she liked to call it, and he didn't quite fit the criteria, although he did tick *some* boxes. These days, though, he *didn't* have to wait for Mad to build up to coming out. George could call on him, and in an instant, he'd be there. What she didn't know was George was in command of his other self now, not the other way around. He'd mastered it, taught himself to be that way, controlling the monster inside him so he kept himself safe and didn't end up in the nick. He'd let her continue to believe Mad was an entity unto himself, the living, breathing beast who pulled George's strings. It'd save her psychoanalysing him more than she already had under the guise of being a couple having a chat. In truth, it was ingrained in her to play therapist even when she was off the clock, something he'd accepted but didn't like. Being silently inspected, her filing away his behaviours and mannerisms, only to bring them out in conversation later, like she'd just done, was a tad creepy to be fair.

Yet still, here he was, with her. If he was so insulted by it, why wasn't he walking away? Why didn't he tell her to go and do one?

"What will you do," she went on, "if you're driving home, see some fella acting as a pimp on Cardigan, for example, and Mad decides to fuck the fact there's CCTV, fuck being careful, and he forces you to stop the car, get out, and batter the shit out of said pimp? There'd be no Greg to warn you to keep driving. Mad would know he had you all to himself—you have to admit, he's a devious bastard. I think in future when we meet up, you should ask Greg to drop you off and pick you up. That way, you're never alone. You're not *safe* on your own, either from Mad or the police."

George laughed. "You think I need my brother to play *babysitter*? Fuck off, love, seriously. And that would be rubbing salt in Greg's wounds. He's only just getting to grips with me leaving him at home when me and you go out for some nosh. You know he struggled with it for a while, letting me go. What about the nights we don't part ways at a restaurant? Do you expect me to ask him to collect me at your place, him knowing what we'd probably been getting up to in the sack? In a lot of areas of my life, I'm a cunt, but not to him. Never to him. Don't expect me to hurt him on purpose, because I'd sooner walk away from you, from this, than use him like that. He's my *brother*, my other half, he's a version of *me* in another body, something no one other than twins understand, and no woman will *ever* mean more to me than he does."

She didn't get all upset, didn't whine and say *she* should be the most important person in his life because, give Janet her due, she understood the twin bond and wouldn't dare to assume she should be in the number one spot in his life, even though some would say she should. While he was catching serious feelings for her, he'd never choose her over Greg. Even if he loved her almost as much as his brother, which he didn't, not yet, he'd still let her go.

"Okay, I see where you're coming from," she said, "and yes, that would be cruel, so maybe get Will or Martin to drive you about in your taxi. I'm not trying to control you, I swear, it's just I'm worried. I know what Mad is capable of. I need you to keep yourself safe from him."

"What are you really saying? Come on, it's not only you who can play the therapist card. I've learnt a lot from my time torturing people, observing mannerisms, tells, and reading human beings to see what makes them tick. Tell me what's eating at you."

"No."

"Why not? Are you scared to?"

She leant forward, eyes flashing, and whispered, "Fucking hell. All right, I care about you. I don't want to lose you. And I mean *proper* care about you. There, I've said it."

Fuck me. Was she saying she loved him? He didn't know how to deal with that. "Right. I see where you're coming from, but love doesn't mean you have carte blanche to control me. Or Mad."

She sighed in frustration. "I *know* that. This isn't what it's about. Let me put it another way."

"Go on then, stun me with one of your little analogies."

"You're being an arsehole. And stalling."

"I know."

She glared at him, clearly contemplating whether she should bother to continue wasting her breath. She wasn't a wallflower who'd stop if she thought she'd pushed too far and Mad was just beneath the surface. She wasn't scared of Mad, something that fascinated George and had him pondering on more than one occasion whether she was just as warped as him. She had to be, to be involved with a bloke like him. She had a set of balls on her bigger than many men he knew, and she wasn't afraid of *either* side of him. That's what he liked most about her. That she accepted him for who and what he was.

Or she had until tonight.

She seemed to come to a conclusion. "Okay, let's try this a different way. Say you had the urge to throw yourself out of a car when it's speeding along."

What the chuff's she on? "You fucking what?"

"Hear me out. It's a known phenomenon. *L'appel du vide*—call of the void. The urge to do something like that comes fast and leaves just as quickly. Some people have other urges. To turn the steering wheel into oncoming traffic. To stand on a platform and jump in front of a train. To dive from a high bridge, knowing that when they hit the water, the force is likely to break their back, kill them. You know these impulsive thoughts aren't what you should do, so your brain saves you at the last minute, stops you from doing it, but you have the urges regardless. It's linked to anxiety sensitivity, where those who suffer from it believe things like an over-pounding heart means you'll have a heart attack. The brain goes into 'oh my God' mode and assumes the worst. If you have anxiety sensitivity, you're more likely to automatically go to the dark side, where you're convinced a minor symptom is something dangerous."

"You went into full therapist then."

"I know I did, but I'm trying to help you to see. Mad *isn't* an urge, like being in a car and wanting to hurl yourself out of it then stopping yourself. You can't control him like you can by remaining in the car and waiting for the compulsion to pass."

"I don't like labels," he said, "so if you're thinking of telling me some name or other which says what's 'wrong' with me like you did before, don't bother. I don't see Mad as wrong."

"And that's where the problem is. You'll never get rid of him if you think like that."

"I seem to remember me telling you, not too long ago actually, that I don't feel like myself when I suppress Mad. That I don't *want* to get rid of him. I thought you understood."

"I do."

"So why try to change me?"

"Fuck me, weren't you *listening*? Obviously not, so I'll repeat my-bloody-self. I don't want Mad to overtake you when you're alone and you end up getting caught because you don't have anyone there to pull you away when you go too far, hence having Martin or Will ferrying you around when Greg isn't there."

"For fuck's sake, I don't need a bodyguard."

"I think you do."

"Then we'll have to agree to disagree."

"I don't want to have to say this, George, but I will anyway. Can't you at least *try* to lay off being so nasty when you torture information out of people? For me?"

He chuckled. "I never thought you'd go down the 'for me' road. Thought you were better than that. Feminine wiles, they piss me right off. They're manipulative. I'm going to sound patronising, but I don't give a fuck: I'm disappointed in you."

"Of course you are, because if you concentrate on being disappointed in me and telling yourself I'm trying to change you, it means you don't have to face the real problem—that you have a fucking mental health issue that needs addressing. Are you part of the Neanderthal man brigade, someone who feels men shouldn't speak up about mental health? Are you going to remain in your non-progressive state, believing all the tripe Richard or Cardigan instilled in you, where you have to be strong and deal with problems like a 'man', using violence as a means to get what you want? How about dealing with them like a human, no gender involved? How about admitting you need proper help instead of trundling along being a monster whenever Mad decides you should be? Whenever *you*, as George, decide you should be."

"Oh, the sodding claws are coming out now."

"Because I *care*."

He smiled. "Is this our first row?"

"If you think so, then I suppose that's what it is, because, what do you know, George is always right."

He sighed. "This is a monumental milestone."

She frowned, her irritation clear. "What?"

"The first row. It means we've moved from dating and sex to something else."

Air burst from her quivering nostrils. "You're deflecting again."

"It's what I'm good at."

She leant back, arms folded. "You really knob me off, do you know that?"

"Yeah."

"You're like a brick wall. I can't get through to you. Your defences are up, you've blocked out the reason I want to help you, all because I think you're afraid to let Mad go. You think you can't live without him, that with him gone, you're boring or not as strong. He's a passenger in your mind, a tenant who lives rent-free and ruins the furniture."

"Don't hold back on the metaphors, will you."

She pursed her lips. "I'm not saying anymore tonight. I know you. It'll percolate, and in the end you'll see I only have your best interests at heart. This isn't about me being manipulative or trying to get you to do what I want. This is so you acknowledge you have to deal with your mental health before it ends up consuming you." She stood. "I'm going to finish our first row by doing the classic storm-out, because that's what's expected, what matches your fantasy of how a relationship goes. And just so we're really playing our parts, I'll finish up by being ambiguous, so you go home wondering where you stand, by saying: see you when I see you, George."

They had another date tomorrow night. He'd bet she turned up.

She walked out, back straight. He caught sight of two taxis waiting outside and her getting into one, so he relaxed, knowing she was safe. The restaurant door closed, ending that particular spat.

He sipped the remains of his Coke. She wasn't wrong, he *was* good at deflecting, and he *didn't* want to acknowledge all the shit she'd said about Mad. In fact, she'd just set things off, Mad chattering in his ear about outwardly doing what she wanted, appeasing her, just shooting victims in the head after an interrogation at the warehouse, but inwardly, under the cover of darkness, Mad could come out to play. Even Greg wouldn't know about it.

George wanted to prove her wrong. He *could* be Mad sometimes and not get caught.

He'd show her.

Chapter Four

Gloves on, George got in their fake taxi in the car park behind the restaurant and drove away, his mind full of the recent conversation. Janet had assured him she wasn't trying to change him, but she was lying to herself—and him. Of *course* she wanted him to change if she'd asked him to control Mad, to basically banish him forever. What else could it be called if not that?

Like he'd said, they'd have to agree to disagree, but it wasn't lost on him that he was willing to end victims' lives in the warehouse with a single bullet to the head instead of allowing Mad to be sadistic, just so she was appeased. He must care about her more than he'd thought, or, conversely, he was falling into the trap in relationships where he was doing it for a quiet life.

That was more like it. Having her going on in his earhole hadn't been pleasant. She was obviously at a point where she'd slipped out of the shiny newness of them being together and into something more comfortable, where she felt she could pick holes in him. He didn't enjoy the feeling he got when people preferred him over Mad, as if Mad was some obnoxious entity who didn't deserve to exist. All right, that description was apt, Mad *was* an utter wanker, but he was part of George's essence, and if he wasn't there, George wouldn't be George. Why couldn't she see that?

Or was she saying he was *enough* as just George?

I don't fucking know.

He had a conversation with Mad all the way back to the East End, and Mad wasn't best pleased about the recent turn of events. Janet would say George having a conversation with an evil part of himself wasn't the same as 'normal' people who nattered to themselves. She'd say those people talked to the person they actually were, not a separate persona. That George had...what had she called that condition the other week?

DID.

"What's that mean?" he'd said.

"Dissociative identity disorder."

"That tells me nothing."

"People with DID aren't sure who they are. They have other identities, with their own names, voices, histories, and ways of behaving. Sometimes, the other entities take over, and the original person has no idea that one of the others has overtaken their lives until they bump into someone who recounts a meeting they've had and the person with DID has no clue what they're on about. Or they get caught for a crime they swear they haven't committed, when they have, as one of their other persons."

"But I know what's what with Mad. I'm still George when he comes."

"Nope, not all the time. There's something called dissociative amnesia, when the person has times where they can't recall what they've done—you've said when Mad comes, sometimes you don't remember what he did. You stare down at a mangled body, a body Mad bludgeoned or whatever, and the act itself is lost on you."

"So you're saying I'm a nutter. A schizoid."

"No, I'm not saying that at all. You can't help what happens. Both conditions are sometimes directly related to past trauma. Think of Richard, what your mum went through with him and Cardigan, what you and Greg went through. Those traumas have pointers that show people like me, therapists and psychologists, how to diagnose."

"What's that then, these pointers?"

"PTSD. Depression. Mood swings—don't tell me you don't have those, because I've seen them myself. You can turn dark in an instant. Anxiety—you're paranoid you and Greg will be split up somehow, that you'll lose him, and you have spates where you're anxious about it. There's self-harm, suicidal tendencies. All right, you haven't displayed those, but you do have what could be considered an eating disorder. At a stretch."

"What?"

"You rely heavily on Pot Noodles—chicken and mushroom, it can't be any other flavour—and sliced tiger loaves with butter. It's a go-to for comfort, and now Greg has adopted the same pattern with the same food. You've unknowingly projected your crutch onto him. You have many points of dissociative amnesia. These are things you can get help with if only you'd let me show you the way."

"What, get stuffed full of tablets? No thanks."

George threw that memory out of his head and cruised the streets of The Cardigan Estate, looking for someone he could take his unsettled feelings out on. This would be his little secret, his and Mad's. He'd become someone else—yet another person to add to Janet's DID theory, fuck it—and blame all these night-time shenanigans on him. What could his name be? George tapped the steering wheel, thinking.

He pulled over into a lay-by and Googled: *A violent person involved in crime.*

The word at the top of the list of results had him smiling.

Ruffian.

"That'll do, donkey."

Except he'd prove her wrong there, too, that he was present at the same time as Ruffian, so he *didn't* suffer from DID.

He drove away again, going into the outskirts, away from home. Prowling. Waiting for prey to appear. On the outer road bordering a housing estate, a row of trees and a field beyond on his left, homes lit up by lights on his right, he clocked an alley that led to the estate. He was still on his and Greg's manor, so he could do what the fuck he liked and, spotting two blokes touching hands in the darkness of the alley, he screeched to a halt and launched out of the taxi, running at them full pelt. One spotted him and bolted down the alley, disappearing, but the other seemed dumbstruck, likely a novice buyer of drugs and unversed in the art of escaping when trouble brewed.

"You fucking twat," Ruffian said in a Scottish accent. "Doing business on Cardigan without permission. I wonder what The Brothers will have to say about that."

"Jesus, I'm sorry, all right?"

"Sorry isn't good enough. You must know the rules."

The bloke backed away, the streetlamp at the other end of the alley turning him into a silhouette. Skinny. Thin. "Who are you, one of their men?"

"Something like that." Wind jostled Ruffian's shaggy wig, sending a strand across his eye, and in the time it took him to swipe it away, the fella had run off.

Ruffian went after him, the burn of Mad searing every part of him, the chase, *this* chase better than any shot of adrenaline. He had free rein, he was on his own, and while it was a tad alien not to have Greg at his back, Ruffian could handle it.

In the street, he caught up with his quarry and gripped the back of his bomber jacket, yanking him backwards, ignoring his yell of protest. The neighbours would probably ignore it an' all, they wouldn't want to involve themselves in any trouble. Ruffian hauled him back into the alley, past the splash of light and into the darkness. He threw him against the side wall of a house, letting him go, then grabbed his throat and shoved him onto the bricks.

"Is this your first time buying drugs?" he asked.

"N-no."

At least he's honest. "It's going to be your last."

The fella nodded as best he could, what with Ruffian's hand blocking his chin from moving. "I swear, I won't buy any again."

"No, you won't."

With no tools at his disposal, no gun or knife on him, he squeezed the twat's neck, pushing his weight into it for a quicker dispatch, knowing he'd have to stand like this for a good while until the bastard died. He stared into eyes going glassy and ignored the hands that came up to slap at him and try to wrench his wrist away. It was pointless, Ruffian had planted his feet firmly in an unmoveable stance, his arm so straight the elbow had locked.

Time seemed to pass in an instant, when in reality, it would have been a few minutes, then the man's distress of dying, the panic to save himself faded, and eventually, his arms hung limp at his sides. This was a shit kill, no hot blood spatter on Ruffian's face, no flesh spewing from a wound, no missing teeth or glued-up cocks, stapled nostrils, all the punishments Mad liked to inflict. This was going back to basics, which was in his favour. If he left his usual hallmarks and

Janine, their copper, got wind of this murder, she'd know it was him. She'd be on his fucking earhole like Janet, and he didn't want that.

In order for him to do what Janet and Greg wanted, he had to let Mad out this way, a delicious, dirty little secret he'd never tell a soul.

The body slumped, and Ruffian held on for a minute longer, just to make sure, then he let it drop to the path. The fella landed on his side, his tongue swollen and hanging out, visible even in the murk. Ruffian glanced into the street, and someone stood there in the shadowy darkness, maybe the other bloke who'd been selling to the pleb on the ground. Then he ran.

Ruffian let him go. He had another idea in mind.

He went to the dark end of the alley and waited for cars. The dead prick must have walked here, unless his vehicle was in the residential street, but for the seller to be standing here, it was obvious people drove this way and bought their fixes.

It didn't take long for a vehicle to slow, its headlights dousing before it parked in front of the taxi. Someone got out, heading towards Ruffian who braced himself for yet another attack on his part. They came closer, slowing, probably checking out his shape and seeing it wasn't the same as the usual seller.

"Mule?" they asked.

A fucking woman? Bollocks.

"No," Ruffian said, hiding his shock. "He's not here tonight. Afraid it's just me. What do you want?"

She moved even closer, an arm's reach away. "Just some sniff."

"Addicted, are you?"

She huffed. "What's it to you?"

Ruffian shrugged. "Just wanted to know how often you buy, that's all. I mean, I could do you a deal; you could come to my usual patch. I'm cheaper than Mule."

"I buy three or four times a week, depends what I'm doing. How much of a deal are we talking, and will I get in the shit with Mule if I switch buyers? I don't want him on my back. He's...well, he can be a nasty bastard when he wants to be."

Ruffian repeated the name in his head — *Mule, Mule, Mule* — in case Janet was right and he went into some kind of fugue and forgot this conversation. He had to let George know to remember it, and then he almost laughed loudly at thinking of himself as Ruffian, as a separate person, proving Janet's theory. No, she *wasn't* right. If he was aware of his other selves, he *didn't* have any of that DID crap.

Do I?

He stuffed a fist in his pocket, pretending to remove drugs, and she held her hand out, cash flapping in the wind. The sound of it annoyed him, the *crack-crack-crack* bringing it home that money was changing hands here on the nightly and George and Greg hadn't known. George would make out he'd had an anonymous tip-off so Greg didn't ask questions, then they'd hunt down this Mule, end the bastard.

Ruffian flashed his hand out and gripped her wrist, dragging her towards him so her chest bashed into his. He clamped his hand around the nape of her neck, spinning her so her back was to his front, then slapped a hand over her mouth, stopping her scream before it had even been a thought in her drug-greedy head.

In her ear, he said, "You've been a naughty girl. You didn't go to any of the legitimate sellers. You came to someone who didn't have permission to peddle. You'll have to pay for that."

He marched her towards the taxi, the driver's door still open from when he'd legged it. She breathed heavily against his pointer finger beneath her nose, the heat of the air warming his skin through the glove. This would have to be the substitute for him having no blood on his face tonight, one of the best things about a kill. The way he planned to kill her *would* spill blood, but his mug wouldn't be anywhere near it.

"Hand me the flick knife in the cubby of the door. If you think about using it on me, I'll twist your fucking neck until it snaps, got it?"

He allowed her to bend her knees enough to ferret in the cubby and bring the knife out. She held it up, whimpering, and he shuffled her over to her vehicle, shoehorning her inside as though he'd allow her to drive away. That's what he wanted her to think. That she'd had a close shave and he'd let her disappear far from here, never to return, to realise the error of her ways.

All bollocks.

He let her go, remaining wedged in the gap the open door created so she couldn't get out. The interior light would show her what he looked like, and she glanced up, no recognition on her features at all. Why *would* she recognise him? He didn't resemble George or Greg.

He was Ruffian, a Scottish ginger man mountain who'd put on gloves at the start of his journey, knowing, before any of his selves had, that he was going to kill on his way home. He flicked the blade out of the knife's handle and placed it against her neck, disregarding her shrill scream.

"Shut up."

She glued her lips closed and stared ahead through the windscreen, nostrils flaring with her heavy breathing. "Please, I have kids."

He should feel bad about that, but he didn't. He'd have to hand it to Janet, she did understand him well. He didn't have control of himself at all times. He *liked* the feeling he got when the control slipped, where he didn't give a single fuck about anything except for what he was doing. He also liked it that he'd truly conquered his aversion to killing women. He could walk away now, let her go free, but he wouldn't. He didn't want to.

"Do you have a fella?" he asked.

"Yes."

"Is he clean?"

"Yes."

"Then stop worrying about the kids. He'll look after them. They'd be better off without a cocaine-sniffing mother anyway." A part of George came striding in: *Think of what the kids will go through. Let her go home. This is enough, she's shit herself enough.*

The swipe of the blade on skin in the direction of the passenger seat was awkward, but it did the trick. Spatter landed on his suit-sleeved arm, coating the top of the steering wheel, spotting the dash and windscreen. Forensic plebs would be able to determine how he'd done it — there was a gap where his arm had blocked the claret's trajectory — but he didn't give a fiddler's. He withdrew his arm at the same time her head fell forward, hiding the majority of the wound. Blood came down in a sheet, a baby's scarlet bib, and soaked into her white T-shirt.

She still clutched the money she'd intended to hand over to him, then her fingers relaxed, opening, the petals of a flower in the glory of the sun, and the five ten-pound notes rested on top of the drink holder between the seats.

He left it there. Left *her* there. Got in the taxi and drove towards home, letting Ruffian go, wondering, as George would, whether he should give Janine a heads-up, then decided not to. After all, he didn't want anyone knowing what he'd done, did he.

This was to prove to Janet he was in control. She'd see that soon.

Chapter Five

*A*lbie didn't like it in the suitcase. The air was stuffy — that's what Mum would have called it — but at least he was warm. Too warm really. His skin, clammy with sweat beneath his coat, prickled, and his lips tasted of salt. He thought about the chips Muttley was going to buy and whether they were for him. They had salt on, but he wouldn't mind that sort.

The motion of the suitcase being carried had unsettled him, then a big swoop where it had probably been lifted and placed somewhere. The thud of what sounded like Dad's car boot had frightened Albie, but at least he had an idea of where he was now, especially when the engine rumbled and it seemed as if they were on the move. He couldn't hear much other than that rumble and the noise the tyres always made if Dad drove in wet weather. Slap-slap-slap. It must have rained since Albie had come home from school.

The journey seemed to take forever, but eventually, the car stopped and went silent. The slam of the car door. The scrape of footsteps. The click-clunk where the boot had been opened. Then Albie was in motion again, someone grunting—it had to be Dad, didn't it—as he complained about the weight. The case must be banging against his father's leg, as Albie was jostled, then a loud creak scared him, and he whimpered.

Finally, the movement stopped. He imagined the case had been put down. The noise of the zip relieved yet scared him, and he closed his eyes, not wanting to see where they were. The lid of the case flung back—he knew it had because light pierced his eyelids, sending them red—and cool air snuck over him, drying the sweat on his face so his skin went all tight.

"Get out, you soft fucker," Dad said.

Albie opened his eyes. Where was he? The place was about as big as his classroom, but it didn't look the same. It only had one table, a chair one side, two on the other, and crates of some sort stood against the left-hand wall. They had wooden lids, and one had a hammer on top. Black bags, like Dad put in the kitchen bin, had stuff in them, but the tops were tied. A tall cabinet with drawers, the top one open a bit, had labels on each one. Albie squinted to read them from this far away but couldn't make out the letters.

"Didn't you hear me?" Dad said in that voice he used when he was nearly angry, when he'd raise his fist and breathe loudly until Albie obeyed. "Get out!"

Albie didn't need telling again. He clambered from the suitcase and hugged himself, squeezing tight to make everything okay again inside him. He didn't like what he thought of as worms squiggling in his belly. They always did when Dad was around, and when things got really bad, they tied themselves into knots.

He glanced about some more, spotting a metal door beside a wall that was well weird. It was metal, too, the same as the sort shops had over their windows when they closed for the night. Were they in town? Was this an empty shop? Albie racked his brain. If he remembered rightly, the toy place had shut down last month. Could they be there?

Someone knocked on the door in a one-two-one tap, and Albie's knees sagged. Muttley walked in carrying a packet of chips. Albie didn't like Muttley, but seeing him was better than seeing someone else. A stranger. What was it Dad had once said? Better the devil you know.

"Get these down your neck, kid." Muttley held them out, shutting and locking the door with his free hand.

Albie glanced at Dad who switched on a three-bar fire by the table. Dad nodded his permission, and Albie ran towards Muttley, taking the hot package that smelled like heaven. It was hot and burnt his palms, but he didn't care. He carried his precious dinner to the table and sat, peeling back the paper. Steam wafted out, and the scent of vinegar hit him in the face. He stared at the contents and looked at Dad again.

"You got him a fishcake an' all," Dad said to Muttley. "Now who's soft?"

"Fuck off." Muttley went over to the fire, crouched, and held his hands out to the orange glow. "I've got sweets in my pocket if someone's a good boy."

"Ah, I get you," Dad said. "Smart."

Albie didn't even want to think about the sweets. They might not be for him, Muttley had said they were for 'someone', and imagining eating fizzy cola bottles or gummy snakes always upset him because he rarely ever got any. But he had chips and a big round fishcake, and that was better than any sweets or the slice of bread he'd tried to nick.

He ate quickly at first, needing to fill his empty tummy, then Dad told him to, "Slow down, you gannet!", so Albie did as he was told. Dad and Muttley whispered stuff over by the door, and with his back to them, Albie could pretend he wasn't in a strange room, that he hadn't been brought here inside a suitcase. If he wanted to end up crying, he could also pretend Mum sat opposite, sharing the chips, but that would be daft and get him sobbing, so he pushed her memory away and concentrated on filling his stomach.

He couldn't fit it all in, hated seeing all those chips left on the greasy paper, but it was okay, Dad came over and crammed a few into his mouth. He pulled a chair out, scraping it on the floor, and sat, leaning forward to pick at the remaining food. Muttley walked over and stood behind Dad.

"This is our office," he said. "It's where we store stuff that we sell on."

Albie remembered Mum saying Dad was a salesman.

Muttley eyed him. "You're going to work for us now you're old enough, but first you need to learn the rules."

Albie was good at that. He knew all the rules at school. No shouting. No bullying. Stand in a straight line in the dinner queue. No peanut butter in your sandwiches because some kids got poorly even if they got a whiff of it. You weren't even allowed Nutella because that *had nuts in it an' all.*

He wanted to know why he'd been put in the suitcase but didn't dare ask. Dad might shout, tell him he was a nosy twat, and Albie didn't want that to happen. Tonight had turned from scary to magical, what with that big dinner he'd just had, and he didn't want to spoil it. He wished every night could be like this moment, where his belly was content and he didn't get sent to bed.

"It's a secret club," Muttley said. "One only special people can join. We think you're special, so here we are. It's so secret that no one but me and your dad can know where the office is, which is why you were put in the suitcase. If you don't know where we are, you can't tell the police, can you."

The police? Albie's stomach rolled over. He was scared of coppers. "I won't tell no one nuffin."

"No, because if you do, your dad will be taken away and you'll be left all on your own."

Dad could be mean, but Albie didn't want to be by himself. He'd be scared and all sorts. And even though he didn't get that much to eat at home, it was still better than the nothing he'd have if Dad wasn't there.

"I'll be good," Albie said.

Muttley gave a quick nod. "I know you will, we'll make sure of it. Now then, this is what your job is. Listen carefully, because it's important you understand exactly what to do if things go wrong, got it?"

Albie bobbed his head, his dinner doing weird things to his belly, although it might be Muttley doing that with his nasty stare and big forehead. His black hair, parted in the middle, was tied back in a ponytail, and his chin had a strip of beard on it the size of a piece of Wrigley's chewing gum. He was so different to Dad, who had shaved hair, brown like Albie's, his blue eyes without that silly shelf on top.

Muttley told Albie what he needed to do. It was wrong, Albie would be in so much trouble if he got caught, but he reckoned if Dad said it was okay, then it sort of must be, mustn't it? Dad always said Albie had to do whatever he told him or he'd get a smack, so it wasn't like Albie could say no. Still, stealing was naughty whether Dad told him to do it or not, but the threat of his father being taken away and Albie being left with no one meant he'd do whatever they said.

"If you do all that," Muttley went on, "I'll give you sweets after every job, and later down the line, I'll give you sweets and money. But not until we know we can trust you."

"You can," Albie said, desperate for the money. He could buy that dinosaur in Tesco then, the one that made weird noises when you pressed the red button on its tummy. It would have to be that. Dad wouldn't let him have the doll which actually wet itself. He'd say it was a toy for girls. "I'll be a good boy, you'll see."

Dad glared at him. "You'd better be, kid."

Muttley dug a hand in his pocket, brought out a big bag of sweets, and tossed them on the table. "You can eat those once you've helped us go through the gear in the black bags."

Albie stood, his stomach distended from too many chips. "Is that my first job?"

Muttley laughed, and Dad sighed.

"Told you he was ready, Steve," Muttley said. "You ought to listen to me more often, especially when it comes to getting rid of women."

The bags contained all sorts, but it was odd, because none of it was in boxes like they were in the shops. Toasters with crumbs inside, laptops with fingerprint smears on the screens, and one bag even had shiny jewellery in the bottom. Albie had to take each piece out and tell them what it was. Dad wrote things down in a big red book at the table, and Muttley took the items from Albie and stored them in the crates. He put the jewellery in little boxes and placed them in the drawers with the labels on the front. Now Albie was closer, he could read the words, although it took a minute or so to work them out. He wasn't that good at reading, not yet. NECKLACES. RINGS. BRACELETS. WATCHES.

With the last bag emptied, Dad called out, "Two grand, give or take a few quid, and it depends whether the gold and stones are real. If they are, we're looking at a damn sight more."

"We've got that big payday coming up, don't forget. Albie will come with us on that one."

"He could fuck it up," Dad said.

"I'll be good." Albie said that a lot, what with the way Dad was, always angry at him for some reason or another. Saying he'd be good meant Dad calmed down a bit. "I can do what you said. I won't mess nuffin up, I promise."

Muttley smiled. "Come on, Steve, you know it makes sense. We can't afford to have this job pinned on us, and we need someone smaller to get inside. It's too big to fuck about and take risks." He looked at Albie. "We'll be the three musketeers, won't we."

Albie didn't know what that was but nodded anyway.

"We'll have us a secret all to ourselves," Muttley said. "You, me, your dad, we're going places. You'll have so many sweets you won't be able to eat them all." He sent one of his glares Albie's way. "But remember, I can take the sweets away as easily as I give them out, and your dad can stop giving you dinner an' all, so unless you want to go hungry, then you'll do whatever we say. Won't you."

Albie nodded again. He'd do anything for a full tummy.

Chapter Six

In protectives, DI Janine Sheldon stood under a bright sun on a chilly day, glad of the extra layer over her suit and thick coat, especially the gloves and mask, her forensic outfit only leaving her eyes exposed. They watered from the cold, but not from the sight of what lay before her. That was her story, and she was sticking to it.

She stared down at a body at the end of an alley on the Bracknell housing estate, one renowned for people on the lower end of the class system, the type who still maintained the old rules of being there for their neighbours in times of strife, lending a helping hand to watch kids or nip to the shop for someone who couldn't do it themselves. That boded well for the door-to-door enquiries, where folks would want to give as much information as possible in order to find who'd done this. She wished the whole world was still this way, having each other's backs, it would make her working life easier, but sadly, the internet, social media, and streaming apps had ensured people had become more insular, those in other areas of the East End preferring to mind their own business and turn a very blind eye.

The dead man, who'd had ID in his pocket in the form of a credit card or two, was Dean Matson, although his address or age hadn't come back yet from whoever was dealing with that back at the station. The poor sod lay on his side, both arms out as if he'd reached for someone, his fingers loose, thin, a gold signet ring on one of them. His tongue hung out, an alarming shade of purple, and where he'd perhaps lost all of his saliva through fear while being killed, white stripes had dried on the side she could see. Or maybe that was some substance or other that had been administered to incapacitate him; he'd maybe swallowed a rape drug, could have been in the local pub with someone who'd drugged him and offered to walk him home.

She could only imagine what had gone through his head prior to death. He didn't appear to be the usual sort of lad who wound up dead. What she meant by that was he didn't look like a gang member, he didn't have a suit on to show his profession or, indeed, an affiliation with a leader who expected him to dress smart, and earlier, at first sight, her sixth sense had told her he'd never been in any trouble.

Her work phone rang, and she swiped to answer. "Yep?"

The sergeant at the station gave her Dean's address and age. "He doesn't have a record, not even the usual shoplifting as a teen, something we see all too often on people's rap sheets."

"Okay, cheers. Anything else of significance?"

"He appears to live with his mum. Both of their names are on the electoral roll at the same residence. He works in those new offices down our way, near the station. Accountant."

"I knew he wasn't a dodgy sort, although saying that, accountants can be iffy."

"Well, that's all we've got."

"Thanks."

She ended the call and pondered. What had Dean been doing here? Why had he been killed? The answer to the first one was easy. He could have been either on his way home from a night out, entering the alley to get to his house on the estate, or he'd left someone's gaff and had been on his way to his, on the farthest part of Bracknell. But with the presence of another victim in a car nearby, a woman, who by all accounts had had her throat slashed, it threw Janine's initial theory into confusion. She hadn't gone to see the female victim yet, the pathologist was in the alley tending to Dean, so she'd made that her first port of call.

A police officer patrolling in his car at nine this morning had logged the deaths. Janine had not long tied up the loose ends of a serial killer case, so with nothing immediately pressing on her hands, she'd been dispatched to attend this scene with a new DS on her team, Radburn Linton, a man of Jamaican heritage who'd fitted right in as soon as he'd set foot in the incident room. She preferred his personality over her old DS, someone who'd got right on her pip, always up her arse, which made it difficult to do things on the sly for the twins.

Radburn stood beside her now, taking down notes that the pathologist, Jim Trafford, was calling out.

"Petechiae surrounding the eyes, a burst blood vessel by one pupil, indicating strangulation or suffocation." Jim gestured. "Further compounding the former, the presence of bruising on the front of the throat with a clear imprint of one hand, the palm, finger and thumb tips. I don't need to tell you this is a strong person, one well able to hold another against the wall and strangle him one-handed for a considerable amount of time."

"That much is obvious," Janine said.

Jim continued. "Unless drugged or knocked into unconsciousness, as you are aware of by now, a victim will automatically fight to get their attacker off them, so unless the killer was well-covered, they would have scratch marks on them. Prior to bagging Mr Matson's hands, though, I had a peek beneath the fingernails, and there doesn't appear to be anything there, like skin, which would yield the DNA results of the person you're looking for. No soil or anything either."

"So he wasn't accosted on the verge then," she said, "then dragged here."

"As far as I know from SOCO, there's no indication around here that he was on the grass verge, no, and there's no mud or anything on his clothing. On the knees, for example."

"So the attack likely happened here, and it's a man we're after."

"Hmm. I don't think it's a woman, unless she's of the high-strength variety. To completely cut off air, the pressure needed is three times thirty-three pounds, so the force created by the person's hold would need to be ninety-nine pounds or over, hence my suggestion the person is likely to be around two hundred pounds in order to have that kind of brute force and stamina to hold the victim for so long. After the trachea is closed off, brain death occurs in four to five minutes, so this person had time to stand here until Mr Matson was deceased—and they were capable of maintaining their grip."

"So someone who wasn't scared of being caught," Radburn said.

"Possibly," Jim replied. "But going by the rigor which has fully set in, we know he's been dead for twelve hours at least. It's ten a.m. now—I'm surprised no one else stopped to see what was going on before the officer spotted the bodies, people going to work and whatever—so it would have been dark at ten p.m., most people at home. Perhaps there *was* no rush to get this done quickly. The murder, I mean. With another victim in the mix, too, this person maybe knows this road well, they know there's not much traffic. Someone could have driven by and seen, I suppose, but why not contact the police?"

"They were too afraid to phone it in?" Radburn suggested.

"I don't believe that," Janine said. "The people around here are a good bunch. Unless it was someone passing from another area, someone of the more selfish variety."

"Or they could have been worried the killer clocked their number plate and came after them next," Radburn said.

"I'll give you that one." Janine nodded. "Maybe it's a duo working in tandem. There are two methods of murder here. Dean's been strangled, and Jim, you mentioned the woman had her throat sliced."

"Highly plausible there's two involved," Jim said, "but I'll collect fibres and whatnot so we can link the murders as committed by one person— or not. For now, I suspect it's a lot of door-to-door enquiries for you two."

Janine shook her head. "Not us. Uniforms are already on it. We've got the grim job of two death knocks, informing next of kin, although saying that, we'll do one, and I'll get my DCs to do the other. I'd prefer the families are informed quickly, without a gap in between." She glanced to the other end of the alley where, on the far side of the road, people stood gawking, their phones out. "We need a tent over him as soon as possible. News of who he is will spread if we're not careful, and their NOKs might find out that way before we have the chance to get there."

Jim nodded. "The tents are on the way. Bit of a snaggle in traffic on the ring road, so I'm told, so they're held up. Five minutes out, apparently."

"Can't be helped," she said.

As the scenes were in the same vicinity, Janine and Radburn kept their original shoe covers on and traipsed over to the car, an old-fashioned beige Mini, while Jim stayed in the alley to change his whole outfit because he'd touched Dean. A photographer had just finished snapping images of the car, the victim, and the surroundings, and he gave them the nod that it was okay to come closer. He walked off, and they stood on the verge, away from the open car door so Jim would have room to work.

Janine stared at the woman whose head was down as if she'd just dropped off to sleep. The blood told another story, though, and the start, or indeed the end of the slice, depending on how the killer had done it and whether he was right or left-handed, peeked out from a curtain of dried blood that had gone down to stain her T-shirt that had BARBIE BABE on it in glittering pink words.

Radburn snorted. "I assume that's in reference to the doll and she isn't a barbecue-loving Australian," he said from the side of his mouth, garnering a hoot of hilarity from a nearby SOCO on hands and knees searching in the grass.

Janine nudged her partner with her elbow. "Gawd, don't make me laugh. You haven't worked with Jim before, and he can get funny about dark humour around the dead. He doesn't feel the need to cover up distress with a good chuckle. Says it's disrespectful. I'm inclined to agree on the face of it, it's a bloody awful thing to do when you think about it, but we'd go mad if we didn't indulge in a bit of banter. Just keep it under control when he's around."

"Got it."

Jim ambled over, carrying an evidence step and his bag of tricks. He placed the step close to the car and stood on it, then fished around in his bag and took out a folded plastic sheet. "Can you put that on the ground and place my bag on top, please? It'd be handy if you do what you did with Dean and pass me my things when I need them."

Jim got on with his usual checks, declaring the woman in full rigor. Her name and address had been gained from the first officer on the scene who'd called in her number plate, and she was Laura Wilson, twenty-eight. She lived on the Bracknell estate but on the other side, which was probably why she'd driven here. What for, though? Had she pulled up, seen Dean being murdered, and copped it herself?

Jim called out his findings, and again, Radburn jotted them down. Once it was clear they were of no further use here, Janine led the way to her car, which was parked a way behind the Mini, and beckoned the log officer who came over and held out bags for their protectives.

In the car, she stared ahead at forensic officers taking casts, probably of tyre treads, where a vehicle—the killer's?—might have been. "What the hell were Dean and Laura doing out here together? Was it an affair gone wrong? Had one of their partners found out they were playing away and followed them, lost the plot, then killed them both?"

"God knows, but we'll get a better insight when we talk to the families. They might not even have known each other."

"True. I did wonder if she came along and saw Dean being murdered."

"Could have."

Janine pulled away, itching to use her burner phone so she could ring the twins. She had to check whether this was anything to do with them, although if it was, George would have contacted her by now, letting her in on the fact she'd need to divert the investigation away from them. She'd do that anyway, just in case, but for now, she'd phone her DCs and tell them to go and see Dean's family. Janine had opted for Barbie Babe because she'd spotted a tattoo on the inside of her wrist that read: MUMMY TO SALLY AND CONNOR. She wanted Radburn to deal with this type of death knock, to watch how he coped with it since she was mentoring him, then she could point him in a better direction if his attempts were ham-fisted, or alternatively, praise him for his delivery and handling of the situation.

She only hoped he didn't fuck it up by mentioning a barbecue in Australia.

Chapter Seven

Aster had slept well at Debbie's, considering. Debbie had a way with words and had calmed her, getting her to think things through logically. Yes, Aster's dad had clearly sent someone out to find her, but if he knew where she lived, he'd have shown his hand a lot sooner. Okay, the man in the car now had an idea of the vicinity of her home, but for all he knew, Aster could have just used that road to get to another one.

Before she'd got up, she'd sent a message to Sarah and Kallie in their WhatsApp group and told them she'd stayed over at Debbie's and would be talking to The Brothers this morning. Their replies had been emojis, smiley faces and hands clapping, and Sarah had told Aster to have a great day, despite what had happened. It was so weird, having friends on the end of the line, ones who'd answered immediately. The other mates she had didn't contact her for weeks on end, and to be fair, Aster didn't contact them either, although she knew she could if she was in a bind. They had lives to lead but would be there for her at the drop of a hat. Still, no sense in bothering them with all this, not now she had Sarah, Kallie, Debbie, and soon, the twins.

The thought of opening up to George and Greg was a daunting prospect. Debbie had said giving them all the information as to why Aster's father was chasing after her, even when so much time had passed since she'd last seen him, would help them to understand the urgency, the danger of Aster's situation. Admitting to some of the facts of the matter to Debbie had been traumatic enough, Aster's part in it when she'd been Albie seeming too awful to repeat, but she'd done it anyway. How could she not when Debbie had been so expert in coaxing the truth out of her?

Aster wandered from the lovely spare bedroom she'd been given and into the hallway. The scent of bacon drifted to her, and voices, Debbie's and someone else's. Someone Aster hadn't heard before. Her stomach churned — he sounded a bit like Muttley — but of course, it wouldn't be him. She shook off her fear and knocked on the kitchen doorjamb in case their conversation was supposed to be private.

"Don't be daft," Debbie called. "Bloody get in here. Want a bacon sarnie?"

Aster entered the room and stopped short at the sight of a big man leaning against the worktop beside the Tassimo machine.

"Morning," he said. "I don't bite. Well, I won't bite *you* anyway." He extended a hand. "Brickhouse."

She stepped forward and shook it, then all but skittered around the breakfast bar to perch on a stool. Debbie nudged Brickhouse away from the coffee machine as if he were an annoying little brother, completely unfazed by the sheer size of him.

"Fucking pest," she said. "Sod off out of my way."

"Charming." He winked at Aster and came to sit beside her. "I hope you're not as rude when I babysit you."

"Babysit?" Aster asked.

Debbie prodded a button on the machine then brought a bacon sandwich over. "Like I said to you last night, or was it the early hours, I can't remember, I told Moon about this after I phoned the twins to arrange a meeting. Moon's loaning Brickhouse to us so he can look after you until they've found your penis of a father."

"Oh. Right. Thanks."

"Have you got a spare room?" he asked Aster.

"Um, yes?"

"Then I'll kip in it. I'll be up your arse twenty-four-seven."

Aster relaxed. With this fella by her side, *on* her side, she wouldn't have to worry about that weird man in the car accosting her. On the other hand, how would that pan out with work? "Err, it won't go down too well with the punters.

They're not going to want you in the back of the car when they're getting seen to."

Debbie carried cups of coffee over, thick foam on top. "You're not going to work. The twins are paying your wages until it's safe for you to go back."

Tears pricked Aster's eyes. She knew all about The Brothers, of course she did, and she'd spoken to them once or twice when they'd checked things were going okay on the corner. She'd heard they could be nice when they wanted to be, but to pay her wages? That went above and beyond. So used to fending for herself, Aster would find it difficult to accept monetary help, it would take her back to the days when she'd had to beg for coins to buy food, but she'd do it. She didn't want to offend the twins by refusing, not when they were taking on her problems with the intention of solving them.

She bit into her sandwich, going into her own world while Debbie and Brickhouse chatted. The clock read ten to eleven, so Aster had overslept, which wasn't surprising, seeing as they'd eventually got to bed about four a.m. She was still tired, and pent-up tension at the prospect of going through everything with the twins,

Brickhouse here to listen to the whole sordid story, tightened her muscles. She'd been loose by the time she'd gone to bed. Talking to Debbie, getting it all off her chest, out in the open, had taken such a weight off her, and to not be judged, to have her actions validated, meant the world.

Like Debbie had tried to get across, Aster wasn't a monster, she'd been controlled and had no choice but to do what she had, and blaming herself would only mean she spent the rest of her life in unshakeable turmoil. The idea that she could come out on the other side of this, free and without such heavy burdens, seemed a foreign concept, but Debbie had shared her own story and, although she'd promised things would get better, she had said the sins of the past never truly went away. She'd warned Aster that it would be a long road to recovery, but it was doable, becoming someone who didn't always think of their bad deeds first thing of a morning and last thing at night.

Bacon sandwich eaten, the effects of a good coffee swirling through her veins, Aster properly joined the land of the living.

"I've got myself a bird," Brickhouse said. "Well, it's early days yet, only been on a couple of dates, but it looks promising."

"How does she feel about what you do?" Debbie asked. "If she's even aware."

"She's part of Moon's crew so knows the score."

"Oh right." Debbie collected Aster's plate and put it in the dishwasher.

"Will she mind you staying over at mine?" Aster wasn't sure she wanted some arsey woman banging on her door and accusing her of stealing her bloke, although she'd like to think Brickhouse had been told not to give out her address. But still…

"Nope. She's not that type. Anyway, this is work, so she can go and do one if she gets funny." Brickhouse waggled his empty cup. "Mind if I make us another one?"

"If you replace the pods," Debbie said. "You've already had two."

"Someone who counts the pods is a sad sack." He grabbed Aster's cup. "Ah, they're here. I'd recognise those clomping footsteps anywhere. Pair of fucking elephants."

Aster listened to the *thud, thud, thud* of shoes on the steel steps outside. Her stomach went over, and she swallowed and breathed deeply to combat her nerves. This was silly, getting all aerated at the thought of seeing the twins when they were coming here to help her, but their reputations frightened her. She'd have to get over it, though.

A knock on the door sent Aster's knees weak, and Debbie went to answer it. The sound of coffee spurting into a cup reminded Aster to ground herself.

Brickhouse glanced at her. "Don't shit your knickers. They're pussycats. Sort of."

"Easy for you to say. I bet you're mates."

"They might come off as harsh at various points, George especially, but it's all for your own good."

She stared at the door. Debbie came in, followed by The Brothers, and their size and auras meant Aster struggled to breathe. Their presence was like nothing else, the air fizzing with it, and she placed her palms on the breakfast bar to stop them from shaking.

"Morning, Aster," one of them said, coming over and giving her a side hug. "George, in case you couldn't work it out. How are you diddling?"

She gulped. "Better now I've got it all out."

He stepped away to drag another stool over and sat by her. "I heard your dad's being a bit of a cunt."

She laughed, his direct approach easing her nervousness. "A bit?"

"Hmm, well, he won't be one for much longer, not once we've got our hands on him. I assume you know where he lives."

She shrugged. "He might still be at the same address, I don't know. I left when I was sixteen and haven't been back."

"Why don't you tell us all about it while Debbie makes me a Pot Noodle."

"Christ," Debbie said. "You're always chancing your arm."

Greg leant on the wall by the door. "Come on then, Aster love, out with it. The sooner we know your full story, the sooner we can find the bastard—*and* the man in that car."

Aster took a moment to form the words she must have said a thousand or more times. "First off, I've got a dick."

George's expression didn't change. "So? What the fuck do we care? And what the hell has it got to do with this?"

She was safe then, with everyone here. They accepted her for her. Tears bulged, and she dashed them away. Why was it, when people took her at face value, she got so emotional?

Because you've had to fight all the way to be recognised as who you want to be.

"I have a number plate," she said and recited it. "I think I remembered it right."

"That's a good start," George said. "We'll get our copper onto it."

"Right. Okay. I suppose I'd better tell you everything, then." She took a deep breath. "How long have you got?"

"As long as it takes," George said. "Get talking."

Chapter Eight

*T*he house was a great big one, and Albie reckoned
a king or queen lived inside. It stood in the
darkness, loads of grass and trees around it, no other
buildings in sight. He hadn't been put in the suitcase
tonight—he was only in there whenever they went
from home to the office—and they'd been in the van for
ages, although it wasn't Dad's, nor Muttley's. Dad
said he'd 'borrowed' it for the job and they'd dump it

later and set fire to it. Albie thought that was a waste, it was naughty to set fire to something, but he didn't say a word.

Dad had bought him some new gloves, and Albie's hands were so hot underneath them, but he wasn't allowed to take them off. He had a hat, too, but it wasn't like any other hat he'd had. If he rolled it down, it covered his face, the eye and mouth holes tight on his skin. Dad said it was a ski mask and that one day, if they hit the big time, Albie might be able to actually go skiing. The Alps, he'd said. On the journey, Albie had imagined all that snow and the mountains, getting excited about having a holiday, something he'd never had. It would be so cold his nose would turn red, his eyes watering.

Dad had parked the van on a long driveway, the back end facing the house, the rear doors open. He and Muttley had ski masks and gloves on, too, and all of them had gone down the side of the house to the back. It was true what Muttley had said on the way here, there was a small window open, one with glass like the bathroom at home, where you couldn't see in or out properly.

"He'll fit," Muttley said.

Albie had been told about this. He had the most important job, they'd said, getting into houses through *little windows and opening the front doors. The first time he'd done it, he'd been so scared, thinking the people who lived there would catch him, even though Dad said they were on holiday. Muttley had a list of places that would be empty, and he knew because he worked somewhere that told him these things. Still, Albie always thought he'd get caught right up until they drove away with all the stolen stuff.*

Albie had always known stealing was wrong. Every time he watched Dad and Muttley cart things out of houses, he was reminded of the colouring pencils and how Miss had been so upset and disappointed that he'd become a thief. What would she think now? While he wasn't nicking anything, he was helping Dad and his horrible friend to do it, so that was just as bad, wasn't it?

There had been someone else who'd done the same as Albie, but they weren't a musketeer anymore. They'd been doing it for a long time, but they'd done something bad, so they weren't allowed to do jobs now. Dad wouldn't say where they'd gone, just that they'd learnt their lesson and he'd been the one to teach it.

"This one's alarmed," Muttley said. "Which is a given, what with the size of it, so as we discussed, Albie, when you open the front door, get out of my way quick so I can turn the alarm off."

95

Muttley always knew the right codes.

Albie nodded, his nerves bunching.

Dad slipped his tool through the gap in the window and unhooked the latch. He pulled the window open as far as it would go and tutted. "Fucking hell, he's never going to get through there. If you didn't feed him so many chips and sweets, he would."

"Shut your face. That's why I don't feed him until after a job. His belly isn't so big then. Like I just said, he'll fit."

Muttley gripped Albie beneath the armpits and swung him up so he was side-on. Albie put his hand inside and grabbed the sill. With him pulling and Muttley pushing, Albie managed to get inside up to his belly, then got stuck. He squirmed against the edge of the window, and something gave with a loud crack.

"The pressure's broke the lower hinge bit," Dad said, "the part that stops it opening all the way."

"Who cares, it means there's more space." Muttley gave another shove.

Albie shot forward, his willy hurting from being pressed to the sill. "Let me go now." He held the sill with both hands and brought his feet up so he crouched. Below was a toilet, so he put one foot on the cistern, the other on the loo seat, then jumped to the floor.

Heart going mad, he approached the door, then turned to look over his shoulder. The window had been closed, leaving a small gap like before, and, as always, he became frightened, as if he'd been left inside to face a monster. He twisted the doorknob and peered out through a small gap. A hallway bigger than his living room. A little red light flashed high up, and he knew enough now that it was a motion sensor. Muttley had told him where to walk so it was less likely to catch him, but if the alarm blared, Albie had to open the front door quicker than ever so the police didn't come out.

He crept out of the loo and sidled along the wall to his right, making his way along that and the next one, slow and steady, like Muttley had taught him. All the while, he stared at the red light, waiting for the alarm to spring to life. He felt sick, but the promise of a chippy tea and sweets pushed him on, not to mention this was the first time he'd be getting money. Muttley said they trusted him now.

The dinosaur he'd buy appeared in his mind, urging him on, and, at the front door, he reached up and pulled down the handle of the Yale. He prepared himself for the wail. Yanked the door open and darted to one side. The alarm kicked in, and Muttley rushed inside, going to the left wall and opening a little white box. He jabbed at the keypad, and the noise stopped.

Albie breathed out, his legs going all funny, then Dad came in and shot upstairs. Muttley ran into a downstairs room, and now Albie had to start his second job, standing at the door to watch for anyone coming. He hated this part, the fear of seeing someone giving him the jitters.

Dad and Muttley worked for a long time. They carted out big TVs, laptops, and two computers. Dad ran backwards and forwards with kitchen appliances, vases, ornaments, and this big statue thing that had stood at the top of the stairs. The van was getting fuller, especially when two rugs went inside, and Albie wondered why they'd be nicking carpets. Surely they weren't worth much, were they?

The men in Albie's life took a 'breather'—Dad's word—in the hallway.

"The safe's in a nook behind a picture in the main bedroom," Dad said. "Keypad, so…"

"Can it be taken out?"

"Yeah, it's moveable, but it'll be fucking heavy."

"Bollocks. Come on, we'll give it a go. There's too much inside it that'll bring in the money. We're not leaving it behind."

They disappeared upstairs, and Albie faced the driveway. Lights from cars on the dual carriageway in the distance went by, but they were too far out for him to worry about it. Besides, the house was in darkness, no one had switched on any lights, so they were still okay.

He stood there for what felt like ages. A loud donk had him jumping, then came the scrape of something, as if the safe was being dragged along the floor. Albie didn't dare turn around to see what was going on, but the great big clatter and thumps of something coming down the stairs told him they'd let the safe fall.

"It's dented the fucking floor," Dad said.

"Who gives a fuck? They'll have insurance."

It wasn't until Muttley told Albie to 'get out of the fucking way, kid' that he stepped aside. They struggled with the safe between them, their gloved hands clutching two bottom corners each, and they shuffle-walked to the van and dumped it inside.

Dad slammed the doors shut and rubbed at his mask-covered cheek. "Job done. Come on, Albie."

Muttley closed the front door, and they all got into the van and sat on the big front seat, Albie in the middle. He wasn't allowed to take his mask off until one of them said so, and it was a while through the country lanes with no one speaking before Dad gave his permission.

"Those rugs alone are two grand apiece," Muttley said.

Dad grunted. "Posh bastards."

Once they neared the lights of London, Muttley put his hand on the back of Albie's head, forcing it to his knees. This was the way it went after a job, Albie not allowed to see where the office was. The pressure released after a few minutes, then Muttley put Albie's ski mask on, but back to front so Albie couldn't see through the eye holes. He was guided out of the van and into the office, the mask fabric getting wet where he breathed, open-mouthed. The click of the door, then the mask was whipped off, and Albie did what he always did and sat at the table with his back to the door. Dad and Muttley got on with bringing the safe in, their grunts and moans worse than before, then came the other stuff.

"I'll go and get our dinner," Muttley said, and the door snapped shut.

Dad sat opposite Albie and passed him one of two cans of Coke. "You can have a whole one this time. You've been brilliant. Really brilliant."

Albie couldn't get over it, the Coke and the praise. It was all a bit much to take in. Tears pricked his eyes. Did Dad like him now? Would he be the same as other dads and play football with him and stuff? Take him to theme parks and zoos like Christopher's father did with him?

"You were a good lad tonight," Dad said. "I'd say I'm proud of you, but that's pushing it bit too far. Remember, this one's going to hit the news, and people will be talking about it because of who the people are who own the house. You say nothing at school, you got that? Nothing."

Albie nodded and struggled to pull the tab on the can. His nails weren't long enough. "I never say nuffin."

"Keep it that way." Dad snatched the drink and opened it. "Fucking hell, talk about butter fingers."

The pleasure from having Coke and praise evaporated a little, leaving Albie curling in on himself.

"If you end up like your mum," Dad said, "well, let's just say you might want to start liking forests, because that's where you'll go."

Forests?

Albie took a sip. The bubbles and burn were the best. He didn't ask what Dad had meant about Mum and forests. Dad always said weird things like that, and the first couple of times Albie had questioned it, he'd got a smack. It was better to keep quiet.

"She was such a stupid cow," Dad went on. "All she had to do was your job, yet she wasn't satisfied."

Albie remembered Mum being little, like a kid. Skinny and short, although she was well pretty, the same as a doll. A rush of missing her pulled at his tummy, and he had to stop himself from crying.

"She had to go, you know that, don't you." Dad sniffed and opened his can. "People who say they're going to snitch, well, they pay the price, and that price is a high one."

"I won't snitch."

"No, I don't think you will, but then again, I didn't think she'd ever threaten to do it either. You think you know someone..." Dad glanced over at the 'goods'. "That's too hot to handle for a while yet. We'll have to sit on it for at least six months, so there's no skiing at the minute."

Albie shrugged. It didn't matter when he went, just that he did. He could wait.

He thought about Mum and what 'the price' was. It must mean that she couldn't come home. Was she missing them? Did she wish she could come back? Dad had been mean to her, too. Albie remembered a few times she'd been slapped round the face, but if she was anything like him, she'd think home was better than wherever she was now, wouldn't she? She must be lonely all by herself. Or maybe she'd made new friends and didn't care about them anymore. Dad had said about snitching. Mum must be really brave if she was going to do that. Dad would go to prison and everything if she told the police.

How come she hadn't done it since leaving them, then? Had Dad scared her into keeping quiet?

Albie pondered that right up until Muttley came back with the food from the chippy. The large man dragged over a posh chair that had been stolen (it had fancy curved legs, red velvet material, and gold studs), and they all opened their packets. Albie had chips and a battered sausage, and Muttley handed out tubs of peas and gravy. Could Albie have some? He wasn't sure and would have to wait to see if Dad said he could, but he really, really hoped he'd be allowed. There were also slices of cake in plastic-lidded trays, one chocolate with foamy icing, one with jam down the middle and a layer of icing sugar on top, and another with toffee sauce all over. It was a big old feast, the biggest Albie had ever had, and he reckoned Dad was right.

This had been the big payday.

Chapter Nine

Steve had a bone to pick with Albie, and he wouldn't rest until he'd got justice. That was the thing about shit from the past. It followed you, nagged for you to fix things. For a few years, he'd pushed Albie out of his head, believing his son would keep his mouth shut about everything, but lately, the little voice in his head had started up again, especially when he thought about

Muttley. Now *that* had been a bad time, and Steve had tried to find Albie after 'the incident', but his search had proved fruitless. Steve didn't care much about anyone except himself, hadn't thought he'd cared about his friend, but obviously, he had. He missed him on jobs. Missed his laughter. But most of all, he missed being able to reminisce with someone who knew about everything he'd done.

So, he was back to finding his boy again. Albie could be his sounding board instead of Muttley. Steve was struggling with keeping all of his secrets inside. It had been too many years, going it alone.

The photos Steve had received from his private investigator, Norton, had shown Albie had gone to the extreme in order to hide, which just went to show how he knew he was in the wrong. You wouldn't hide yourself like that if you were innocent, would you?

He was dressing as a *woman*. Fair play, it was a good disguise, which was why it had taken so long for Norton to track him down—bloody months, it had been—but no son of Steve's was allowed to parade around like that, and it had to be stopped. To top it off, Albie was working on a street corner, earning money for having *sex*.

Fucking little bender.

Steve clenched his teeth and thumped the wall in the living room. The nearby black-and-white canvas of London Bridge swung from the movement, a picture they'd stolen years ago but he hadn't been able to shift when he sold stuff on. Not only had his son fucked off and left him and Muttley in the lurch, he'd ended up as gay as Steve had suspected him to be. That was another thing that had to be stopped. Steve knew this bloke who could smack the gay right out of you, and once Albie was back at home where he belonged, the treatment could begin. It wouldn't cost much, the mate was doing it more as a favour, but it would be money well spent.

By the looks of the images and the reports back from Norton, Albie was still a tiny thing, well able to climb through windows. Steve needed him to help out with jobs again. The last kid he'd used had grown too big, plus he'd stolen some of the goods from the office—an expensive necklace and matching earrings—and had been caught selling them at a pawnshop; the owner had been on the lookout for the items, recognised the seller, and phoned the rozzers. The lad had been in trouble with them before, on his last warning, and this time had been sent down for eighteen months in a youth detention place. He hadn't served that much, though. Two weeks in, and Steve's mate's son, also in the same place, had encouraged the kid to kill himself.

Steve didn't like loose cannons, and although the lad had kept Steve's name out of it with regards to the robbery, it would have only been a matter of time before he'd blabbed to someone in the nick, boasting about his criminal career. It was a risk Steve hadn't been prepared to take, and what was one more murder on his list anyway?

He paced, annoyed Albie had got away from Norton last night. Steve had been *so close* to having him brought in. Albie had walked off with two women, then they'd gone their separate ways, the friends to The Roxy, Albie to the flat above The Angel. Norton had opted to go into the nightclub and seek the girls out, but in the dense crowd, he hadn't found them. The plan had been to interrogate them and find out where Albie lived. That really bugged Steve. Why the fuck hadn't Norton followed Albie home before now and discovered the address? It must be to keeping coining it in, charging Steve the daily rate.

In the end, Norton had staked out the pub, but with no Albie appearing, he'd buggered off home, aborting the mission.

Angry about that, Steve had given him a stern warning, but Norton hadn't flinched.

"I'll find him again on the corner," he'd said. "Don't sweat the small stuff."

"The small stuff? That boy of mine has been gone for years, and when you finally find him, you let him go."

"Don't try to gaslight me by making out I've only just worked out where he is. I found him a couple of weeks ago, remember, and you *told* me to leave it, then last night, you said I had to capture him. I tried and failed, but there's always a next time."

"You don't even know where he lives, which is piss-poor work on your part if you ask me."

Norton had sighed, clearly annoyed. "Because at first, once I'd located him, you said to just watch him on the corner, which I did." Another sigh. "If we have a problem here, you can settle the rest of your bill now and I'll sod off. No skin off my nose, mate. You can go to the fucking corner *yourself* and haul him in."

Well, *that* was a stupid suggestion if ever there was one. "No, he won't come with me."

"He won't come with *me* either, not now. I scared the shit out of him, I could tell."

"Then wear a disguise."

"Fuck off."

Steve had given him a few more choice words, and he swore, if Norton didn't come good this time, he'd kill the bastard.

The memory burned, and Steve punched the wall again. The canvas leapt off and landed on one corner on the floor, the back resting against his drinks globe. Everything seemed to be going wrong just when it had appeared to be going right.

He left the living room, grabbed his coat off the newel post, and paused to stare at the wall opposite. It had looked different once upon a time until he'd cleaned it and given it a fresh coat of paint. God, that had been a bad night, one he wished had never happened. But it had, and now he had to live in fear of being caught. The police solved cold cases all the time, didn't they. It'd be just his luck they'd solve his.

He checked in his pocket for a second set of keys and smiled. As well as this house he had a flat, unoccupied at the moment, in between tenants, and that pissed him off an' all. No extra income from the rent, and he lost out because he had to pay the council tax and TV licence regardless, the latter because he'd been going there to think, the telly on in the background. It wasn't even his responsibility, the flat belonged to someone else.

He left, slamming the door behind him, then winced because it would bring Mrs Greaves two doors down scuttling out the front to have a chat. He didn't need the hassle, but he only had himself to blame.

He made it to halfway down the path, thinking he'd got away with it, then:

"Any sign of Albie yet?" she said, her voice reedy with old age.

She must be about ninety by now, the nosy old bat. "I told you, he *chose* to leave, so why would I look for any sign of him? He was sixteen and within his rights to go."

"But it's so weird. You were just about to go on holiday. And he's your *son*, Steve. It's one thing to let your kids live their lives but another to not care where he's gone."

"I do care" —*he owes me*— "but I won't force him to visit. If he wants to, he'll come back, but if he doesn't, that's his lookout."

"You could have grandkids by now."

"I don't think so somehow." He unlatched the gate, eager to get away from her.

"Well, you just don't know, do you."

"No, I don't." He walked to his car and opened the driver's-side door. Got in, not responding to whatever else she'd said. She could think him rude for all he cared, but he was sick of her rubbing it in his face all these years that he didn't know where his own boy was.

"But you're wrong, you bloody bitch," he muttered. "I know where he is, I just can't get to him yet."

He drove to the flat and went inside, glad it no longer smelled of the person who'd once lived here, the owner. A few tenants between then and now had seen to that, plus he'd paid some bint to come and clean it two weeks ago when the last renter had left. It reeked of cleaning products, and he couldn't seem to shift it. He'd advertised for a new tenant but hadn't had any bites so far, probably because he was trying to cash in on the London prices and was asking a tad too much in their eyes. He didn't think it was too much, the place was furnished, and it wasn't like it was scabby either. On the contrary, it had been trendy when he'd taken it over and could still pass as a decent gaff all these years later.

He prowled the rooms, thinking of how he could do Albie's conversion therapy here instead of at the house. At least that way, Mrs Greaves wouldn't see his son and ask a million questions. He was pleased with himself for thinking of that, and the flat next door was also empty so no one would hear Albie's screams, although Steve planned to gag him anyway.

He sat on the leather sofa, stuck the telly on, and hoped Norton would come good in collecting Albie without causing a fuss. He'd already had a go at the bloke for mounting the pavement in the car and potentially creating a scene—of all the stupid things to do, for Pete's sake—but Norton hadn't seen the problem. If they weren't so late in the game, Steve would employ someone else, but he was too close now to not only teaching Albie a lesson in family loyalty but ensuring he wasn't gay anymore.

"The fucking little twat has got some grovelling to do. You don't just run out on your father, do you, especially not when I've given him a good life."

He grumped for a while, then rested his head back and closed his eyes. He didn't have a job on until tomorrow night, and he'd have to do it alone, what with Muttley not being around and that lad unable to help these days. It would mean Steve breaking a window by the back door of the property and hoping there were keys in the lock. If not, he'd have to smash a larger window in the kitchen and hoist himself inside, all a pest—and risky if an alarm went off—although he'd staked the place out and reckoned it was a false alarm case out the front below one of the bedroom windows, the flashing red light only there to deter burglars.

He knew all the tricks.

Sleep pulled at him, and he succumbed.

Why not? There was fuck all else to do, was there.

The sound of the sea had always calmed Steve, and it was a good job, too, considering what he was doing. Up on the cliff with Muttley, in a thick stand of trees in the middle of a forest, they dug and dug until Steve's palms blistered. He cursed the fact he hadn't bought some gloves, the sort with tough material that meant he wouldn't get sore. He'd left little Albie at home, asleep, and hoped he'd get back before he woke. Still, the boy was used to being left alone, to waking and finding his parents gone. He'd fetch himself some cereal if he was hungry come daylight, and anyway, it wasn't like he had school. The summer holidays had rolled around, contributing to Steve's nerves being pulled so tight he'd snapped last night—Albie was a whiny little prick who got on Steve's tits. His mother hadn't seemed to mind their boy growing into a wimp, another black mark against her.

Steve had done the unthinkable. Tell a lie, it was thinkable, he'd thought about doing it for a long time, he just hadn't expected to see it through. It was one thing to ponder, but to actually do it...

Still, it was done now, and as his mum used to say, you can't change the past, only learn from it. What Steve had got out of this was that he had to control his temper, not let it get to boiling point. He'd warned the missus enough, though, hadn't he? He'd said what might happen if she pissed him off too much. She'd found out the truth of his words, and now look, he had to bury her at the seaside, then he'd have the dodgy job of telling people she'd left him for another man, putting up with all the rigmarole that went with it. The questions, him acting the injured party, when in reality, she'd threatened to expose him for what he did to earn a living — not only him but Muttley, too. She'd been in it up to her neck as much as they were, so she'd have had to confess to the police her part in it, but what had got Steve the most was she'd been prepared to do it.

Prepared to get put inside and leave Albie in the hands of others until they all came back out. What sort of mother did that?

Now, because of her reckless thinking, Steve and Muttley were without an accomplice, and it had put a spanner in the works. They had houses lined up, rich for the picking, and with no one to climb inside through the smallest of windows — usually the little loos — there was a greater risk of being caught.

"You could use Albie." Muttley grunted and chucked a shovelful of dirt onto the growing pile.

"He's too young."

"Then we'll keep going it alone until he's old enough." Muttley speared the shovel into the grass beside him and leant a forearm on the handle. "Do you reckon her parents and friends will believe she just fucked off and left Albie?"

"I've got no other choice but to hope they will. She was unstable anyway, they all know that. She'd threatened to fuck off and cut ties long before she met me. It won't be too much of a stretch for them to swallow my story."

"If you hadn't lost your rag, you wouldn't be in this mess."

Steve stopped digging. Muttley had been throwing out these kinds of jibes ever since Steve had killed her, and it was naffing him off. "Don't you think I know that? And what do you suggest I should have done about her threats to phone the police on us, eh? Let her? Fancy spending a stint in the nick, do you? Fucking hell, I was watching your back as well as mine, and this is the thanks I get, you ungrateful bastard."

"I'm not ungrateful, we could have just done it a different way."

"How?"

"Cut off her tongue and fingers. Made out she'd been attacked. She wouldn't have been able to speak or write then."

"No, they'd have found a way for her to write with her toes or summat. The amount of places we've hit over the years, the amount of shit we've nicked... We'd be looking at going down for a long time. We go in armed, for fuck's sake, just in case someone's home. That's a fifteen stretch in itself, and times that by how often we've done it, we'd lose the best years of our lives in a cell. I had no choice."

"I see your point, but murder? Fuck me."

They continued digging in silence until the hole was about four feet deep. Steve would have preferred six, but it had taken them a fair old while to do this much, and time was of the essence. He tromped back to the car, opened the boot, and stared at her.

He shouldn't have used a knife, especially not in the back garden of a house they'd been about to burgle. Fine, the blood had soaked into the grass, and rain was due, so by the time the homeowners returned from their holiday, there'd be no evidence anyone had been stabbed, but he could have at least waited. He could have strangled her at home, a much cleaner kill, but she'd said she'd take her gloves off inside the target home and touch as much as she could before she opened the front door to let them in. She'd wanted the police to find out she'd been there—and they'd match her prints because they were on the database from when

118

she'd been arrested for theft before Steve had met her. Rage so great had encompassed him, and before he'd had a chance to think it through, the knife had been sticking out of her stomach.

He looked at her blood-soaked T-shirt, how the stain had spread into the shape of Italy, a claret boot with a slice in the middle that showed exactly what he'd done. He should have left it at the one stab, told her this would be her final warning, then taken her to hospital, but she'd have told the nurses he'd done it, so what was the point? With Muttley ranting on in harsh whispers about this being the end and they were fucked, panic had taken over Steve. He'd yanked the knife out and slashed her throat.

He pulled his thoughts way from that and concentrated on what he had to do next.

"Help me get her out of here," he called over his shoulder.

Muttley arrived at his side, and together they lifted her out and carried her to the hole. After a count of three, they dropped her inside, and Steve stood at the foot of the grave, his mind going to weird places, like imagining all those bugs eating her, worms slinking into her ears and nostrils, her mouth, gorging on her eyeballs.

"Shouldn't we have put her in there naked?" he asked.

Muttley sighed. "And take evidence on her clothes back with us? What the fuck would we do with them?"

"Burn them?"

"No, if she's ever found, this way it'll look like she'd come here for a holiday after she left you, and some randomer killed her."

"I don't intend for anyone to find her."

"Then you need to go and gather up some twigs and whatever to scatter over the grass once we've filled the hole in."

Muttley had come up with the idea of being careful to cut into the grass, like you bought turf, so they could lay it over and make sure there were no visible joins. Steve reckoned there would be anyway, at least for a while, so the twig idea was a good one. He didn't imagine anyone would walk through these woods and notice the difference, but best to be sure.

They'd put safeguards in place, using a false number plate, one of many they owned, and had driven here in balaclavas, despite that looking odd if it was picked up on any cameras. Steve planned to set the car on fire in Dolby Field once they got back anyway, then walk the rest of the way home.

All this because she wouldn't do as she'd been told.

Stupid fucking cow.

Steve woke and stretched. He felt out of sorts, had a bad feeling in his gut, but that might be because of the dream he'd just had, one that had recurred ever since he'd killed her. It came once a month or so and, add the *other* dream he regularly had now, and he had broken sleep at least three times a month.

He should have done what Muttley had suggested years ago and moved away with Albie—still in London, just not in their area. A clean break. Too late now. The second incident at his house meant he'd be staying there until the day he died. Much as he'd tried, he wasn't daft enough to think he'd got rid of all the evidence, and while it might look nice and clean, underneath there would be proof of what he'd done.

Yeah, Albie needed to pay for his actions, to help Steve assuage all the anger he'd accumulated since his son had run off. Well, it wouldn't be long, and Albie would be here in the flat, trussed up, taking his medicine.

Steve smiled. Sometimes, life really was worth living.

Chapter Ten

George and Greg stood outside Aster's father's house. George had hammered on the door a few times. The bloke was out or he wasn't answering. Either way, they'd catch him when he finally showed his face. Will, one of their men, currently sat nearby in an unobtrusive car and would remain there until tonight when Martin, their other most trusted, came to relieve him. They weren't giving the bastard a chance to get away, not after what he'd put Aster through.

George knocked again.

"It's pointless," Greg said on a sigh. "He's not in."

"Fine." George turned to walk down the garden path.

"Can I help you?" someone called.

George stopped and glanced across at an old dear with a pink cardigan wrapped double-breasted, her skinny arms clamping the fronts shut. "You might well be able to, love."

She squinted. "I may have bad eyes without my glasses on, but you're The Brothers, aren't you?"

George smiled and made his way to her gate, Greg following.

"We are," George said. "We're looking for Steve. Have you seen him?"

"Why don't you come in for a cuppa. The kettle's just boiled, and I could do with a nice chat. I get lonely, see." She stared at them to convey her true meaning—she was saying that for the benefit of any neighbours listening.

George glanced at Greg who nodded.

"Lonely?" George said. "Well, we can't have that, can we. A cuppa would be lovely."

They followed her indoors, her home surprisingly modern, no remnants from past trends in sight. George had expected antimacassars and doilies, the smell of lavender or piss instead of the freshness of washing powder that scented the air from a tumble dryer giving it some in the corner of the dining area in the kitchen.

"Have a seat," she said.

George and Greg sat with their backs to the wall.

"You shouldn't let people in your house willy-nilly," Greg said. "We could have said we were the twins, could have been lying."

"But I *know* who you are. My husband used to work for Cardigan."

George perked up at that. "Who was that, then?"

"He was known as The Blade."

The name rang a bell. "Ah."

"There used to be parties. You two were called in to run a message once. I never forget faces. I'm Ida, by the way."

Greg crossed his arms. "Do you live with anyone?"

She poured boiled water into a teapot. "No, my husband died twenty years ago, and my kids live in Somerset. I do all right by myself, thank you very much, so don't go fretting. Her next door looks out for me anyway. Gloria. Nice woman. Her boys nip to the shops and whatnot. It's Steve you've got to be wary of. I don't know what it is about him, but he's up to something, always has been ever since I moved in. Living with a man like The Blade, you learn to spot things."

She brought a tray over, teapot, milk, sugar, and cups on top. She placed it down and sat opposite them.

"Help yourself. Now then, if you're here, I can imagine you already know Steve's a rum one. What's he done? Is it about young Albie? When he went missing, well, that night was so odd. The boy legged it up the street carrying a black bag, and I just knew he was running away from home in the proper sense. Steve said he'd moved out, but as a parent, wouldn't you have helped him, given him a suitcase at least? Saying that, the suitcase that was on the doorstep might have been the only one they owned."

George knew what that was about, the suitcase on the step, but he needed to know what the woman was aware of. "Suitcase?"

"Hmm, Steve said him and Albie were going away for a little holiday, but I don't know, something about him was iffy, especially when Albie ran off and Steve went away regardless. Maybe they'd had a row, but it wasn't right. You know when you get a sixth sense?"

Greg nodded and poured the tea. "So how long did Steve stay away for?"

"A couple of nights. Said he'd be going to the seaside. It's just, the suitcase was a really big one, more than you'd need for two nights, and when he lifted it into his boot, it seemed to weigh a ton."

George wasn't about to give anything away. The less this woman knew about Aster's involvement in things the better. He added milk and sugar to his drink and stirred. "We know Albie, and that's why we're here. He wants to make contact with his father but wasn't sure what kind of reception he'd get." A few lies wouldn't hurt. Besides, they were necessary in order to keep Aster safe and for this woman not to alert Steve that something sinister was going on. She may well understand the code of the estates, what with being married to one of Cardigan's men, but at her age, he didn't want to put her in the middle of this, put her in danger.

"Oh, he's always been blasé about Albie going off like that, like a sixteen-year-old running off is perfectly acceptable. I disagree but understand why the lad might have wanted to distance himself. I mean, the times Steve and his mate went out late at night and didn't get back until the early hours. Shocking."

"What do you think they were doing?"

"Going up the pub is my guess. Maybe to a club afterwards or something. Would you like a cake?" She got up without waiting for an answer and took a tin out of a cupboard. She returned to her seat, removing the lid with her wrinkled fingers, and plonked it on the centre of the table. "Made them myself. None of that shop-bought rubbish."

George took out a rock cake with a splodge of jam on top and, after biting into it, he was immediately transported back to his childhood when Mum used to bake if she had spare cash for the ingredients and enough money on the gas meter for the oven. His eyes threatened to leak, and he cleared his throat. "Nice, this."

"My great-grandchildren love them." Ida picked one out and munched on it.

Greg kept his hands in his lap. "Mum used to—"

"Yeah," George said, "she did. Have one. It won't hurt." What he'd meant was it wouldn't dredge up all those horrible feelings they shared, but he was lying. "Not too much anyway."

"Nah, you're all right." Greg drank tea instead.

"So, Ida." George swallowed and leant back. "What else can you tell us about Steve? What car does he drive?" They could have asked Janine to find that out, but with what Ruffian had got up to last night, George wanted to give her a wide berth for as long as he could. The plate number Aster had given them for the other man's car had been a fake, so they were no closer to finding him.

"It's a blue one, a big SUV type. The number plate usually ends in five, eight, two."

"Usually?"

"Hmm, sometimes it's different. When I'm up in the night, on account of my bladder, you know, it's not the same one. This is why I said he's up to something. You don't change your plates if you're being good, do you."

George stuffed the rest of the cake in his mouth.

"Have you ever pulled him up on it?" Greg asked.

"Have I buggery. I don't want him knowing I'm watching him. Once I have something concrete to go on, I'm calling the police."

"Don't," Greg said. "We'll handle things."

Ida's sparse white eyebrows rose. "I see." She tapped the side of her nose. "I shan't say a word."

George contemplated nicking another rock cake but talked himself out of it. "Do you know when he'll be back? If you watch him a lot…"

"He doesn't usually go out during the day, which is a bit odd in itself if you ask me, so him doing it today piqued my interest. And because he's broken his routine, I don't know when he'll be back."

"Has he had any strangers coming to visit lately?" George was thinking of the bloke in the car, the one who'd scared Aster.

"Not that I've seen. He used to have someone coming round, a fella with a ponytail and a stupid thin beard, but funny enough, he stopped visiting a while after Albie ran away. Since then, no one visits Steve. Do I need to worry?"

Greg drummed his fingers on the table. "No. There's one of our men out there in a car who'll wait for Steve."

George scratched his ear. "We'd appreciate it if you could phone us an' all, when Steve gets back." He dug in his pocket for his wallet and handed her fifty quid. "That should help keep you sweet."

Ida took her glasses off the table and slipped them over her eyes, inspecting the cash. "No need to take that tone with me, young man, I know full well how this goes. One, I wouldn't say anything because of who you are, and two, I want Steve caught for whatever he's up to. You shouldn't be here to pave the way for Albie to come for a visit. Steve doesn't deserve that lad. You should be hauling him away and getting some answers out of him, because I'm telling you, he's a dodgy one. I'm right, aren't I?"

George nodded. "Keep it under your hat, though, eh?"

Ida smiled. "I didn't come down in the last shower, boy. Now then, drink your tea and get to work." She paused. "Then come back when it's all over and tell me what he's been up to. It's been bugging me for years."

Beards slapped on in readiness for George's other plan which had nothing to do with Aster and everything to do with Ruffian, he drove away from the street in their pretend work van.

"What do we need disguises for?" Greg asked. "What are you up to?"

"I got a phone call earlier when I was in the loo at Debbie's. Someone called Mule has been a naughty boy on the Bracknell housing estate."

"Doing what?"

"Selling gear."

"For fuck's sake."

"Two people have been killed." George stopped himself from smiling. It felt wicked to keep a secret from Greg, but his need to prove Janet wrong was stronger than sharing what he'd been up to.

"Who?"

"Buyers."

Greg ferreted in the glove compartment and took out a lemon sherbet.

"Giss one of them," George said.

Greg sighed, unwrapped it, and popped it on George's open mouth. "Who phoned you?"

George tucked the sweet against his cheek. "Anonymous, but it was a woman."

"Are the police there? At the crime scene?"

"Dunno."

"And you think it's a good idea for us to go to Bracknell without checking in with Janine first? Jesus Christ."

"Phone her then, mardy arse. Blimey." George would have to let him do it or it'd look suss. Greg would want to know why George didn't want Janine in the know.

Greg got on the blower and put it on speaker. It rang for a good while. Janine must either be ignoring them or finding a safe place to speak.

She answered. "I've just left a house after giving bad news. Can't talk too long. Got a new DS."

"Awkward," George said.

"It could be. He's diligent."

"Where is he now?"

"Still inside waiting for the FLO to turn up. I could do with speaking to you two anyway. Do you have anything to do with a double murder on Bracknell?"

Greg glanced at George, his eyebrows hiking. "No, it wasn't us, but that's why we're phoning. It's to do with drugs, and we're after a bloke called Muse."

"*Mule*," George said. "Get it right."

Janine breathed heavily. She was probably walking out of earshot of the house. "Is he the killer?"

George could hardly say *he* was or it'd send Greg into more of an arsey mood. "My source just told us Mule sells drugs and two people have been killed."

Janine sighed. "Do you need me to stall things at my end?"

"Just until we've caught up with him, yeah." George crunched on his sweet.

"Are you *eating* in my earhole?" Janine sounded disgusted.

George grinned. "Might be. I just want to give him a severe warning about selling without our permission."

"A warning?" Janine sniffed. "Are you going soft? That's usually banishment or the Thames."

"I'm feeling generous today."

"Makes a change. Okay, I can give you twenty-four hours. Once that's up, I'm going to have to make a move on him myself. His name hasn't cropped up yet, not that I know of, but you can bet it will. The people on Bracknell are being spoken to, and one of them will drop him in it if it's him. I can't not follow that up, so it might be inside the twenty-four hours if I have my seniors wondering why I haven't actioned for him to be brought in. And if you end up going too far, at least let me know. Have you got a real name for him?"

"No. Where did the murders take place?" Greg asked.

She gave them the location. "Steer clear. The police are all over it. House-to-house is going on in the three closest streets, so you'll be safe for now in other areas of the estate, but soon we'll have to widen the net."

"We're not stupid," George griped.

She grunted. "Bloody hell, I have to go. The FLO's here."

The line went dead.

Greg put the phone away. "At least your source wasn't lying. We're better off going home and putting puffa jackets on. If anyone clocks us walking around in grey suits and red ties, it's obvious who we are."

"Already thought of that. Trackies and hoodies are in the back."

Greg twisted to stare at him. "I thought you said you got the phone call at Debbie's? We'd already left our place by the time you found out about Mule, so we wouldn't have put clothes in the back."

Fuck it. "I brought a bag just in case we needed them for the Aster lark."

Greg settled back in his former position, and George could have kicked himself. He wasn't used to keeping things from his brother, and he'd have to learn to be more careful. He wasn't prepared to tell him about being Ruffian until he'd proven his point to Janet, otherwise Greg would try to talk him out of it, as usual.

"My foresight paid off," George said. "It's like Ida said: You know when you get a sixth sense?"

"Whatever." Greg huffed. "Pull over here so we can get changed."

George smiled. They'd find this Mule fella and fuck him right up, but George didn't plan on handing him over to Janine afterwards.

They got out of the van and hid behind it to slip the extra-large clothing over their suits and switch their posh shoes for trainers. Back in their seats, George eased onto the road and headed for Bracknell.

"Have we got time for this?" Greg asked. "Steve could be back any minute, then we'd have to shoot over there and pick him up. We can't afford to let Aster down, not when she's been through so much shit."

"If we're in the middle of something with Mule, Moon can help Will out."

Greg folded his arms. "This had better not be a wild goose chase."

"We'll find Mule, don't you worry."

"And what's the plan?"

"The Thames."

"Again, we'd be cutting it fine. Torturing then chopping him up takes time." Greg took out another sweet. "I suppose you want one an' all."

"I wouldn't mind."

George smiled and drove on, planning and scheming. This little side act was turning into a right old laugh.

Chapter Eleven

*A*s the years had passed, Albie had remained small like Mum. Wiry, some would call it. At thirteen, he'd long since realised his father wasn't a salesman. Not the legitimate sort anyway. A false number plate on, he sold things from the back of his car, touring the estates, a regular Del Boy, and Albie had listened in to many a conversation between Dad and Muttley that revealed people ordered things before they'd even nicked them. That explained the toasters and kitchen appliances, then. The rugs.

The family home had changed from when he'd been little, the furniture nicer (some of it stolen goods Dad couldn't shift for love nor money), the carpets decent, the place nice and tidy because Albie did the housework. He still hadn't got over Miss thinking he'd stolen those colouring pencils and had written those horrible things, but she was in his past now, seeing as he was at secondary.

It was a minefield, that school. Bullies homed in on anyone different, and Albie was so different. He didn't do rough and tumble, didn't join the lads to kick a ball about. Instead, he wandered around alone, preferring it that way. He had to work hard to put up the pretence that he was happy inside his own skin. He wasn't, he hated being a boy, but if he told anyone how he felt, they'd rip the piss out of him. Call him gay. Assume he fancied lads, when in fact, he didn't fancy anyone. He just wanted to be himself, the one deep inside him, but with the kids at school and a father like his, he had no chance. Mind you, it could seem as if he fancied girls. He stared at them a lot, wishing he could be like them, out and proud about who he was. He wanted long hair and their clothes instead of his short brown tufts and the jeans and sweatshirts he was expected to go around in.

Maybe one day he could embrace everything he was, but not while he lived under Dad's roof. Dad didn't like 'poofters', and he'd called Albie that many times. Albie had tried to act tough, to be who his father wanted him to be, but it went against the grain. Didn't feel right. As did climbing through small windows and standing watch while Dad and Muttley stole people's prized possessions.

With age had come clarity, but Albie was too far in to back out now. Yes, he could leave, but where would he go? Thirteen wasn't any age to be gadding about by himself, and if he went down the route of dobbing Dad and Muttley in to the police, his life wouldn't be worth living once they got out of the nick. He'd contemplated many times where Mum was, and from the snippets Dad had let slip since that night in the office, Albie suspected she'd been killed. Murdered for not wanting to do her job. It proved one thing. Dad hadn't loved her, and he didn't love Albie either, because Albie was under no illusion that he'd disappear the moment he told Dad he couldn't do break-ins anymore.

Unless he saved up all the money Muttley paid him, Albie wasn't going anywhere, but maybe, in three years, he'd have enough to break free. If he didn't spend much on clothes and shoes, by the time he was sixteen, he could make a break for it. Steal some jewellery out of the drawers at the office just before he legged it. Sell it, get himself a bedsit. What would he do for a living, though, and would it be enough to pay London's prices?

It was something to think about.

Tonight was a Friday and another big haul. Muttley had discovered a house down Stratford way that would be empty for the next two weeks. The owners were on their yacht somewhere hot, according to him, sunning themselves in places Albie would never get to go. The skiing trip had never happened, nor had the promises to go to Spain and 'live it large', as Dad had put it. Albie never trusted anything that came out of his father's mouth now, brushing it all off as lies and manly bravado. He never trusted Dad to keep his hands to himself either. Two or three times a week, Dad's fist shot out and hit Albie in the gut, on the jaw once, but the resulting bruise had his teachers asking questions, so Dad had been careful since.

Dad didn't like him, it was plain to see in the way he behaved in front of Albie. Maybe Albie reminded him of Mum too much, of her 'betrayal', so every time Dad looked his way, he saw red. Albie felt much the same these days. When he stared Dad's way, he saw a man who'd denied him a mother, a man who'd made a decision to get rid of her, all because she'd wanted to do the right thing. How had he persuaded Mum to join him on the theft nights? Had she been frightened into doing it? Or had she gone in willingly at first? When had she decided enough was enough, and had she carried on doing it while she'd got up the courage to tell Dad she wasn't doing it anymore?

It was getting more and more difficult to remember her now. Albie wasn't sure if some of his memories were manufactured by him, a kid desperate to cling to the ghosts of the past, ones that always gave him comfort when they floated by, gossamer-thin and intangible. What he did know was how kind Mum had been to him, how her cuddles had felt, how her perfume smelled like unconditional love. How her singing had lit him upside, and when she'd let him sit on the bed while she'd put her makeup on, she'd told him what all of it was for and which colours suited her best. Blues for the eyes, pale pinks for the lips, and peach blusher on the apples of her cheeks. She'd allowed him to play dress-up, her long clothes swamping him, her high-heeled shoes so big he'd fallen over more often than not, but they'd laughed, and she'd told him he was a princess, and he'd never felt so himself in all his life.

"Don't tell Daddy you put on the dresses," she'd said. "He'll be angry."

Albie swiped away a tear. God, he missed her. He used to feel her presence, even though she wasn't there, but with the passage of time had come a big fat eraser that had scrubbed the house clean of her. He'd since learnt that presence was called hope, him hanging on to the idea she might breeze through the door any second. The loss of that hope had been a big blow when he'd been ten and Dad had slapped his face for mentioning her and asking when she'd be home.

"She'll never be home, d'you hear me? Never. So stop mooching around after her, because there's no point. She made her decision, and that meant she gave you up. I told her, I said, 'Janey, if you want to walk away, you leave Albie. Is that what you want?' And guess what she said, eh? 'I can't do this anymore. It's wrong. We'll get caught. You need to be stopped. It's not right what you're doing.' Like I said, kid, she wanted to snitch, and that couldn't happen, fucked if I'm going in the nick, so she made her choice, and it wasn't you."

Those words had stung more than the slap, and Albie had raced up to his room and flung himself on his bed. He'd cried long after the front door had slammed. Earlier on that hateful evening, Dad had mentioned going to meet Muttley in the pub. Albie had dried his tears and gone into the small box room where all Mum's stuff had been packed up into black bags and cardboard boxes. He'd found her makeup, her dresses, her shoes, and took them to his room for comfort, and he'd found the perfume that was love and sprayed it on his pillow, not caring if Dad came in and smelled it. Albie had been angry, lost, and desperate for some kind of connection to his mother, and each night for a week, he'd brought her things out from their hiding spot beneath his bed and hugged them.

Until Dad had caught him.

Albie never saw those things again. The spare room had been cleared out while he'd been at school one day, every trace of Mum wiped from the house. He'd become someone who internalised everything, keeping his emotions locked up safe, and he'd tried to be the son his father wanted. The façade had held him in good stead apart from the odd slip when the words 'gay' and 'faggot' came out of his father's mouth, but from ten to thirteen, Albie had survived by feeding his soul all of his memories and hoping that one day he'd find his mother.

Now, he shook his head of everything to do with her and focused on the job at hand. He stared at the window at the back of the big property, listening to Dad's and Muttley's heavy breathing behind him. Albie was just about small enough to still fit through a toilet window, but thankfully, this evening it was a bigger one. Dad jemmied it open, pulled it wide, and bent to give Albie a leg up.

Inside, Albie had a nose around before he opened the door. In a large living room, photos sat on a mantelpiece, and he didn't have to squint to see them because Muttley had said the lights came on with an automatic timer to give the impression the family was still at home. A man and a woman with their little girl smiled back at him, and while they were obviously rich, or richer than Albie would ever be anyway, his stomach cramped at what he was about to be a part of. Stealing their stuff. He thought about their reaction when they came home from their holiday, the sense of violation they'd experience, how afraid the girl would be that nasty men had come in here and taken her toys. Yes, they could be replaced, but that wasn't the point.

Albie was a square peg in a round hole with the musketeers. He didn't belong anywhere. One day, he vowed he would belong, although that seemed too far into the future at the moment. For now, he'd do his job and open the front door. It wasn't like he had any choice, was it.

Dad brought a woman home a week later. She was so much like Mum that Albie had thought it was her to begin with. His breath had caught, and he'd automatically gone to run into her arms, then realised she had a bigger nose, the wrong colour eyes, and was a few inches taller and wider. The crushing upset still swarmed through him now as they sat at the kitchen table eating dinner. Dad had laid it out nice, a tablecloth, napkins, the lot, and ordered an Indian to be delivered. Albie was surprised he'd even been asked to join them, plus he had a small glass of sparkling wine, very unheard of.

Dad had been playing a role ever since he'd let her in. A kind father. It was so far removed from the usual that Albie was uncomfortable, waiting for the other shoe to drop. It wouldn't last long, this niceness, it never did, and he wasn't foolish enough to believe Dad had suddenly turned over a new leaf.

"Karen here is a receptionist at the doctor's," Dad said. "I met her when I went in about my manky toe."

Albie cringed. Dad's toe had been disgusting, oozing pus after he'd dropped something heavy on it during a theft night and the nail had cracked, an infection setting in.

"It's all better now," Karen said and stroked Dad's arm.

Albie gulped some wine—he'd need it to get through this meal—and remained quiet. Besides, if he spoke, Dad would get arsey. Before Karen had arrived, he'd warned Albie to only speak when questioned. Albie had assumed someone else would be coming, an associate of Muttley's or something, not some woman who ate like food was going out of fashion. Tikka sauce settled at the side of her mouth and slowly dribbled down her chin. He was surprised Dad hadn't barked at her to wash it off.

"Whoops! Always have been a mucky eater." She used a napkin to dab herself clean then necked the rest of her wine.

Was she nervous? And what the hell did she see in Dad? All Albie saw was a bully, albeit one who'd dressed nicer than usual, his hair recently shaved, and he didn't smell too bad either. Some kind of deodorant.

"Karen's going to be moving in," Dad said as if his bombshell had been anything but. "The surgery she works at has high-end patients, if you catch my drift,

so she's going to be giving us addresses and taking a cut."

That was a surprise, bringing someone else in on the scheme. It had been the three of them for years, breaking and entering, so this new development occurring was a shock. Albie wanted to ask about whether Muttley was in agreement with this but didn't dare.

"We need to move away from the people associated with Muttley's job," Dad said, as if he'd read his mind. "He's got a new boss who's noticed a pattern about the houses we've hit for all these years. The last manager was a bit of a thick bastard and took no notice, just processed any claims, but this one...well, we'd better get savvy. Don't want to get caught, do we."

Albie had thought Muttley worked for the alarm company, seeing as he always knew the codes, but it sounded like he was in insurance. Maybe he had a friend at the alarm place who helped out. Albie no longer cared. His head was full of Karen who now gobbled up an onion bhaji, grease coating her lips. What would it be like with her here? How would things change? Would she be nice to him or treat him like Dad did? Would she clean the house and do the washing? Would she cook proper dinners instead of Albie having to do his best in the kitchen? So much had been left to him once he'd got older, Dad using him as a skivvy. It would be good to finally have a break, to be a kid instead of this teenager who had too much on his shoulders, not only in life but what was going on inside him, the changes puberty brought, the fear that one day Dad would find out he wanted to be a girl.

"How do you feel about that?" Karen asked. "I mean, you've been with your dad on your own for a long time, so it's bound to make you unsettled."

Dad stabbed a chunk of chicken with his fork. He held it up and waved it, a glob of sauce splatting onto his plate, sinking into the tri-coloured rice. "Doesn't matter what he feels about it. I pay the rent, not him. He'll like it or lump it."

No change there, then.

Albie had the urge to say he was backing out of his job, that he wouldn't do it anymore, he'd live somewhere else, but that wasn't on the cards. Until he could get away, he was trapped.

"Fucking answer her, then!" Dad shouted, breaking his fake façade, revealing who he really was for a moment.

"I don't mind," Albie said, heart hammering.

"See?" Dad beamed at Karen. "He hasn't got a problem with it, so you can stop worrying about him now."

She'd been worrying? That was nice. She must be a decent sort if she had Albie on her mind in all this, although saying that, if she was supplying Dad with addresses of rich people's houses, she couldn't be on the level. He fretted about her knowing too much, that he was the one who got inside homes and opened the front door. What if things went wrong with Karen and she ended up moving out, telling the police everything?

Albie's stomach churned.

What if she ended up like Mum?

Chapter Twelve

Brickhouse had driven Aster around for a while.

"What's going on?" she asked, a little nervous, even though she was fully aware he could be trusted. It was two o'clock or thereabouts, so she'd spent plenty of time with him to get his measure. Still, she'd relied on herself all this time since leaving home, and meeting new people and relaxing with them was always hard for her.

"Just making sure we don't have a tail," he said. "The bloke from last night might have been hanging around outside The Angel, waiting for you to turn up for work on the corner."

As far as Aster had seen, the car hadn't been there and neither had the scary bloke, but she supposed he could have switched vehicles while she'd been at Debbie's.

"Oh right. Anyone following?"

"Nah. He must have gone home after you went off with your friends last night."

The journey continued in silence. Aster couldn't let herself relax yet, not until Dad had been found. All these years, she'd waited for this day, and now it was here, it felt surreal, like it wasn't happening to her. Except it was, and she had all the feelings to prove it. Fear, anxiety, wondering if The Brothers would catch him, take him out of her life, and then she could breathe easily.

Soon, Brickhouse pulled up to her flat. "Stay put while I scope the street out."

He left the car and walked up and down, always within viewing range of where she was, then came back.

"Come on," he said.

Nervous, Aster looked around herself, just to be on the safe side. Seeing nothing out of the ordinary, she followed him into the building, him with a gun in one hand and a holdall in the other, the former disconcerting and a relief at the same time. He chose the lift to go up to her floor, and once it arrived, he held a hand out for her to remain inside while he checked the landing. A wave given for the all-clear, she stepped out and fumbled with her key in the lock, anxious, desperate to get inside where it was safe.

At last, they were in her hallway, the door shut. Brickhouse put the chain on and double-locked the Yale. He went off to snoop around, then returned, nodding.

"No one's here. I've brought my Xbox. Mind if I set it up?"

"Fine by me. Do you want a cuppa?"

"I wouldn't mind a tea, thanks. Err, which bedroom is mine?" He held the holdall up.

She pointed down the hall and walked into the kitchen, leaving him to it. While she listened to him going round the flat again, she flicked the kettle on and pondered the conversation at Debbie's today. Aster was emotionally drained from having to recite the highs and lows of her sorry life so far, her limbs heavy from tiredness. The twins had assured her they'd find her father and take him to the warehouse where she could speak to him if she wanted to, get some answers, or at the very least, a sorry. What was the point, though? Dad was never sorry about anything, and he wouldn't think any of it was his fault.

She made the tea and took Brickhouse's into the living room where he was setting up the Xbox. Teacup on the coffee table, she wandered into her bedroom. While she was on leave from work, she'd catch up with some washing, thankful she didn't have cleaning to do because she always kept things nice and tidy. She grabbed a bundle of dirty clothes from the wicker bin and took it into the kitchen.

A knock at the door had her pausing midway in putting a white load into the machine. "Brickhouse?"

"On it."

She stood at the kitchen door still clutching the washing, peering down the hallway at

Brickhouse going to the peephole, her heart beating too fast.

"It's a woman," he whispered. "Blonde hair. Know anyone like that?"

It took a moment for Aster to think, to get her acquaintances into some sort of order. Some girls on the corner were blonde, but none of them knew where she lived. Then there were her two mates from her old stomping grounds, but she couldn't imagine them being over this way without texting her first, and again, they didn't know her address. They understood Aster's need for privacy and solitude. Could it be Sarah, her new mate?

"Let me just check WhatsApp a sec in case someone's got hold of me to say they're coming round." She went back into the kitchen, dropped the washing on the floor, and grabbed her phone off the side.

No messages.

Phone on the table, she walked up the hallway to budge Brickhouse out of the way. A quick peek through the spyhole confirmed her suspicions. "It's a new friend, one of the girls I met last night. Sarah. God knows why she's here, though."

"Maybe she's just being nice and seeing if you're okay. Do you want me to check what she wants?"

"I'll do it, it's okay."

Brickhouse leant against the wall. "I'm staying here until I know it's all right."

Aster opened the door and smiled, even though she didn't want to deal with a visitor.

Sarah nosed inside, spotted Brickhouse, and reared back in jokey shock. "Bloody hell, you're a big fella, aren't you." She winked at Aster. "You didn't say you had a boyfriend."

"I don't! He's staying here for a bit because of…you know."

"Hmm, good idea."

Aster didn't want to be rude, but… "Um, what are you here for? Sorry if that sounds blunt, but I don't usually encourage visitors so…"

Sarah delved into her big handbag and brought out a share packet of Maltesers and a small posy of pink flowers. "Thought you could do with cheering up."

She handed them over, and Aster took them, passing them to Brickhouse who had his hand outstretched as if he was eager to check if there was something hidden in the petals.

"Thanks," Aster said, choked up by the kindness. "I'd ask you in but…"

Sarah flapped a hand. "Don't be daft. We can have a natter here, then I need to shoot off. I met an old friend from school in The Roxy last night, and we're going on the lash later. Takes me hours to get the old slap on and do my hair, so I won't hang about long."

Aster looked at Brickhouse who nodded reluctantly and disappeared into the kitchen. Aster went out onto the landing and closed the door enough to leave a little gap, keeping it open with her backside. While Sarah was nice enough, Aster didn't trust her, not yet.

"So did you go to work today?" Sarah asked.

"God, no. The Brothers have told me to stay off until they sort things out."

"Glad you went to them. I said to Kallie it's a bit weird, that bloke coming after you like that. Have you seen him since?"

Aster shook her head. "We've not long got back. What about you? Got the day off yourself?" It was awkward, the conversation stilted on Aster's side. She just wanted to hole up indoors and forget the world.

Sarah nodded. "Yeah. Pulled a cheeky sick day. I had the hangover from hell earlier. Too much vodka."

Aster had never got drunk. She couldn't allow herself to become vulnerable. Her life was work and home, nothing else.

The triangle light above the lift lit up green, pointing upwards, meaning someone was either on their way to this floor or going higher. Aster instinctively moved back, opening the door wider. She was tempted to call for Brickhouse and ask him with her eyes to end this conversation for her.

Sarah smiled. "Well, I'll leave you to it."

She turned and walked towards the lift, leaning on the wall beside it. The doors slid open, and that man from the car shot out, gun raised, a finger to his lips. Aster froze, willing her feet to move, a scream caught in her throat. Sarah darted into the lift and kept her hand on the door to stop it from shutting, and she wouldn't look Aster in the eye. Why wasn't she hitting him from behind? Why keep the door open?

Aster, mute from shock, dithered on what to do, but the gun aimed in her direction made up her mind for her. She stepped backwards quickly, the handle on the front door slamming into the wall, and she opened her mouth to finally let out that scream.

The man lunged, gripped her top, yanked her forward, and dragged her across into the lift, muttering, "I was warned you'd be trouble." He held Aster in front of him, one arm across her middle.

"What the fuck?" Brickhouse shouted, advancing towards them, in the process of drawing his own gun.

The man pressed the business end of his to Aster's temple and shouted, "Back the fuck off if you know what's good for you."

The doors closed, a shot going off on the landing, and Aster yelled, hoping someone on another floor would hear her as the lift descended.

"I'm sorry." Sarah stared at Aster's reflection in the steel doors. "He made me do it, okay? Said he'd go after my family if I didn't do what he wanted."

Aster closed her eyes, hurt and betrayed, and, despite fear thrumming through her, she told herself it would be okay. It had to be. She hadn't come this far to be caught at the last hurdle.

Brickhouse would make it down the stairs in time to meet the lift, which lurched to a stop, sending her tummy into a somersault. She opened her eyes. The doors swept open, and the man shoved Aster out into the main lobby, the sound of Brickhouse's footsteps on the stairs loud and echoey, the squeak of his soles sharp.

"Get outside and don't say a word." The bloke jabbed the gun to her temple harder.

Too afraid to scream now, Aster stumbled down the two outer steps, wondering where Sarah was. He hauled Aster along to a van with the side door already open, threw her inside, and shut her in. She'd landed on her front, and one hip barked in pain. Undeterred, she got up, turned, and hammered on the door panel with her fists, her knees hurting from the ridges in the steel floor. A gunshot went off again, and she prayed Brickhouse had hit his target, but her abductor jumped into the driver's seat and sped off.

"Fucking silly cow didn't stay out of the way like I told her," he grumbled.

Aster stared into the front of the van. A wire mesh of squares separated her from him. There was no way she could reach her fingers through enough to poke him in the eyes, and a glance around told her the back of the van was empty, so no weapons.

"What's happened?" she shouted.

"I shot her, didn't I. Serves herself fucking right. Anyone who says they're a friend and agrees to take money off a stranger to do what she did deserves all she gets. There's no loyalty these days, but then you'd know all about that, wouldn't you, *Albie*."

Aster ignored the mention of her old name and walloped the side of the van again, determined that someone would hear her, take down the number plate, and call the police. She stopped, made a move to get her phone out of her pocket, then remembered she'd left it on the table in the kitchen. Brickhouse would have memorised the plate, wouldn't he? The Brothers would ring their copper, and she'd find the van.

It'll be okay, it'll be okay...

In the meantime, Aster continued slapping the door and prepared herself for the hell she was sure awaited her.

Dad.

A glimpse out of the windscreen showed her exactly where the driver headed. The streets were familiar, ones she'd walked in the darkness of early mornings, desperate to remain hidden. The street for the flat came into view, the place where she'd holed up and kept herself safe after she'd run away from home. The sight of the high-rise brought on a stab of nostalgia, memories flooding in of her days there. It had been the ideal way to lick her wounds and regroup.

The driver must enjoy mounting pavements. He drove across the one closest to the high-rise then gunned it across the grass, coming to a screeching halt. He dived out, his footsteps pounding, then the side door flew open. He reached in, grabbing Aster before she had a chance to scoot back out of his way and make life difficult, to stall for time so Brickhouse could catch them up. He wrenched her outside, marching her towards the foyer doors, the hard press of what she guessed was his gun digging into the small of her back. He kicked at the heavy glass door, pushing her through the gap, then let her go. The momentum sent her sprawling onto hands and knees, and she scrabbled to her feet, turning, ready to run back outside and barrel into him so he fell and she could get away down one of the alleys between this block and the one next door.

She gaped at the sight of Brickhouse striding towards her abductor, gesturing for her to get out of the way. She darted to the stairwell, closing her eyes and listening to the sounds of a scuffle outside. Grunts, a "Fuck you!" from the man, then a gunshot. She prayed Brickhouse had taken him down and, opening her eyes, she stepped forward to peek outside. The van drove away, and Brickhouse lay on the grass, staring at the sky.

A grip on her T-shirt from behind had her choking as the front of the neck hole was pulled against her throat. She lifted her hands in an attempt to dig her fingers between the material and her skin to get some breathing space, but it was too tight. Propelled backwards, she let out a strangled cry, hoping someone in the ground-floor flats would come out to investigate. Either no one was in or they'd remained inside because of the gunshot. The *ting* of the lift arriving had her stomach lurching, and she knew who had hold of her now. Dragged in reverse into the lift, she struggled to catch a breath, her lungs bursting. He turned her around so her back was to the doors and she could see him.

It wasn't Dad.

Chapter Thirteen

*Karen had been living with them for three years.
Albie was sixteen and had had a taste of what it
was like to have a mother figure in the home, which
was why he hadn't already run with his savings. He
felt he needed to stay in order to watch out for Karen,
to make sure Dad didn't hit her. Mind you, Albie
probably wouldn't step in and say anything anyway,
he was too afraid of the outcome, and the shame of*

being conditioned by his father burnt a large hole in his psyche. Women the world over were strong, they stood up for themselves, so it wasn't because Albie was a girl inside that prevented him from sticking up for himself, or Karen, if it came to that. Even if he'd been a true boy he'd still be scared.

Karen was kind, if a little rough around the edges, nothing like Mum who'd had an elegant air about her despite being brought up common (Dad's words). Karen seemed to care about Albie and what was going on in his life. She asked how his school day had been and whether there was anything he needed to talk about. And the best bit, although frightening at the same time, was she knew who he was inside, said she'd guessed not long after she'd moved in, but she'd promised not to tell Dad.

"Who you are is your business, no one else's. It's only your conscience you need to worry about, and if your soul sings that you should have been a girl, then that's what you should be." She'd paused. "Only once you move out, obviously, because your father... Well, we both know what his views on it are."

Albie had an ally, albeit mainly when Dad wasn't at home. Karen was different when he was there, attentive to him, doing whatever he said, the same as Albie. He thought about how they were careful not to talk about anything 'incriminating' if Dad was due back. Karen didn't want him coming in and catching them discussing Albie's private things.

"He told me not to mother you, to toughen you up instead, but I like you just the way you are," she'd said. "I don't understand how a man can recruit his own child, and so little, too, to help him break into houses, but he's not someone you can reason with. I found that out too late, and now I'm stuck."

She'd clamped her lips shut, clearly knowing she'd said too much, but at least Albie had got the measure of things from what she'd said. She knew who Dad was, she understood more than she let on, yet she was still here.

Why?

Lately, she'd seemed different with Dad, somewhat cagey, on edge when he was around. Albie scoured his memories to see if Mum had acted this way, and he reckoned she had. Jittery, swift glances, the picking of fingernails, the biting of a bottom lip. He recognised the signs because he displayed them himself. People who were at ease didn't behave like that. People who had nothing to fear didn't jump when the front door opened, dropping whatever was in their hands.

"I'm stuck, too, but more than you are," Albie had said. "Even if I ran away, he'd find me."

"Being here without you would be so much harder." She'd sighed and stared out of the window. "But you mustn't hang around for me—I know that's what you're doing, so don't deny it. It's crackers to think I'm still here when I've kept my flat, but he...he's got me right where he wants me. I've told him about posh houses, listened in when people are sitting in the waiting room, told him when they're going on holiday. He said if I open my mouth he'll make sure I lose my job. I should never have agreed to do it in the first place."

"Why did you?"

"Because he seemed dangerous and exciting. I'd just lost my parents, I was lonely. I thought he was someone different to who he really is. I reckoned a bit of thieving wasn't so bad, not when he said he was like Robin Hood, stealing from the rich to provide for the poor. He sells what he nicks at a fraction of the price you'd pay if it was brand-new, and I stupidly told myself he was doing so many people a favour, taking some of their worries away."

"He's making a packet out of their situations," Albie had said. "Him and Muttley always have money on them. Dad isn't Robin Hood, he's just a greedy bastard."

"He reeled me in all right, and now look."

Dad would be back from the pub soon. Karen was ironing in the kitchen, and Albie did his homework at the nearby table. The scent of washing powder puffed up in the steam from the iron, and evenings like these were as close to living in a normal household as Albie would get. He'd be sad to leave now, to say goodbye to Karen, but he wouldn't miss Dad who still viewed him as an anvil around his neck. If it wasn't for the jobs, Albie would have no position in the pecking order. He'd be a nobody, useless, and he'd bet Dad would have kicked him out on his sixteenth birthday if he didn't need him to squeeze through windows.

The key going in the front door had Albie glancing at Karen to check her reaction. She stiffened, the iron going still, then she breathed out and continued pressing one of Dad's T-shirts as if everything was okay. It wasn't, not by a long chalk, and he wondered whether they'd had a to-do before he'd come home from school and she anticipated round two. Karen only worked until three o'clock so was already home when Albie turned up. Dad was usually out with Muttley.

Dad's footsteps had Karen sucking in a sharp breath, and her uneasiness transferred to Albie, his nerves lighting on fire. He bent his head and continued doing his maths—no point in giving Dad something to moan about straight off the bat, saying something like: "Get your homework done, shit for brains!"

His presence seemed to fill the air, to dominate the room.

Albie still didn't look up.

"What's for tea?" Dad said. "I'm bloody starving."

"I've had a stew in the slow cooker all day."

"It'd better have dumplings."

Funny how Dad had once relied on sandwiches, easy snacks, or whatever Albie could cobble together before Karen had come along, yet now he was dictating about fucking dumplings. He'd soon got used to the easy life with her around, as had Albie, because she'd taken over the housework and the washing, saying it was her job now. She was a good sort, was Karen.

"I put those in when I got home," she said. "They've had a couple of hours so should be just about done."

"They'd better be."

Dad thumped out, probably going to his drinks globe in the living room, the ancient thing still taking pride of place. Karen hated it, said a hostess trolley would be nicer, but Dad had waved her suggestion away. He did that a lot, showing her she had no say in things. Albie always felt sorry for her. The pair of them were ruled by a domineering man who thought the world revolved around him.

172

Karen finished the last T-shirt, put it on a hanger, and got on with packing the ironing board away. She left the iron on the side, walked over to the cupboard, and took three plates out, her eyes shiny. What was she thinking? That she regretted ever getting involved with Dad? Did she wish she could just put her things in a suitcase and walk away? Only she couldn't, because Dad had her over a barrel.

"Want some help?" Albie offered.

"No, no, love, you're all right, but thanks for the offer."

He closed his maths book and popped it and his pencil case into his rucksack. School finished next week, and he was annoyed he even had to do homework now his exams were over. He'd enrolled in sixth form, although he still looked like a year eleven, a skinny short-arse, and wished he didn't have to go. Wished he had an escape route he could take without guilt piling on top of him. He could go now, but not if it meant leaving Karen behind. Would she be receptive if he told her they could hatch a plan to run off together?

Karen dished up the food, so Albie laid the table — he had to do something, she couldn't do it all. She gave him a grateful smile, and a tear plopped out and down her cheek.

"I wish you were mine," she said quietly. "All mine. Then I could—"

He paused in putting a fork down and stared at her. "What, your kid?"

"Hmm." She nodded and placed a dumpling on a plate. "I can't have children."

"Oh." He didn't know what to say—to what she'd just said or to her wishing he was hers. No one other than his mother had given much of a shit about him his whole life, so to have someone who cared... The lump in his throat hurt. "I wish I was an' all," he whispered and geared himself up to jump in with both feet. "Then we could run away."

Her hand stilled the serving spoon, and she whispered back, "For God's sake, don't let him hear you say anything like that."

"I wouldn't be here if it wasn't for you," he said, low. "I'd be long gone. I've only stayed because you're here."

"But you don't have any money or anywhere to go."

"I've got money."

She seemed to relax then, as if knowing he had an escape fund had her feeling better.

Albie pressed on. "You've still got your flat, so you could go back there if you…if things aren't good here. Hide there until you can move somewhere else."

She flinched. Shook her head. Morphed back into the happy Karen she dredged out from deep inside her when Dad was home. "Come on then," she said, loud and bright, "let's get this dinner eaten. Steve! It's ready!" She took three cans of Coke out of the fridge and popped them on the table, then went back for the plates and set them on the placemats.

She didn't sit, she waited for Dad to come in, and once he'd taken his seat, she lowered onto hers. The dynamics had definitely changed. She'd become subservient, a woman who deferred to her fella at all times, and it just about broke Albie's heart that someone who'd once been so vibrant, funny, and full of life had had the spark snuffed out of her.

I hate him. Hate everything about him.

Dad dug in, shovelling food into his mouth despite the steam coming off it. He always boasted about his 'gob lined with steel'. He had fists of steel, too, all of him coated in the hardness of metal, a rigid man without an ounce of sympathy inside him, although he'd done a good job of pretending he had a soft centre when Karen had first come on the scene.

All gone now.

Albie chewed some beef. "This is lush, Karen."

"Thank you." She smiled and popped a carrot in her quivering mouth. Swallowed. "It's the Oxo cubes. Always does make a nice gravy."

"Tastes like any other stew I've had," Dad grumbled. "No better than the supermarket ready meals. In fact, they're better, and that's saying something."

Karen seemed to inflate with...what? Indignation? Hurt? She clamped her lips as if telling herself not to retaliate, but it was obvious the devil on her shoulder had given her a big old prod and egged her on to defend herself. "If it's not to your satisfaction, there's a Sainsbury's down the road and a microwave on the worktop."

Dad glared at her. Albie's stomach hurt.

"Did you just say what I thought you said?" Dad roared. "Did you just tell me to go and get my own dinner? Why the fuck would I do that when I have you at home?"

Karen's cheeks flushed, and it was as though a light bulb had gone off inside her, lighting her with the flames of courage. "D'you know what, Steve, I'm sick of this shit and I'm sick of you. Cook your own damn meals and do your own housework in future, because I'm out of here."

Dumbstruck, Albie stared at her pushing her chair back and standing, then at his father whose mouth had dropped open to reveal the chewed food inside. Albie's heart hammered wildly. Had what he'd said to her earlier given her the final push to walk out, and Dad being an arsehole had added to her crazy leap into danger? Albie mentioning the flat must have prodded something to wake up, something that had lain dormant since Dad had wrung all the life out of her.

She marched to the kitchen door and paused, looking over to Albie. "You know where I'll be, love." Then, behind her hand at the side of her mouth so Dad couldn't see, she mouthed: COME WITH ME.

Dad dropped his cutlery and stood. He inflated, too, but it was anger that filled his veins and bunched his muscles, the tic in his jaw showing Albie that the shit was about to hit the fan. Dad glanced around, snatched up the iron, yanking the plug out of the socket, and stormed over to Karen whose eyes widened as the iron swung through the air towards her, the flex flicking, an angry snake. The metal part landed on her face, and she screamed at the same time that Albie cried out "No!", and he swore her face hairs sizzled from the heat of the iron plate.

Karen groaned and staggered backwards into the hallway, out of sight, and Dad followed. The grunts and screeches propelled Albie to his feet, and he rushed around the table to stand in the doorway. Karen was on the floor, Dad at her feet, bent over, whacking her head with the iron over and over. Karen stopped making a racket, stopped fighting, yet still Dad beat her with his weapon. Blood spurted, and with every lift of the iron, it spattered on the cream wall, a thousand and one specks. Albie didn't move to stop Dad. He couldn't. His legs wouldn't work, but most of all, if he stepped in and tried to stop him, Dad would turn on him next.

The shame of saving himself burnt Albie to the core, and he let the tears fall as Dad stepped away, into the living room doorway, and stared at him.

"This is the high price you pay," he said. "So now you know."

Chapter Fourteen

It hadn't taken long to find Mule's gaff. Some kind—or frightened soul, whatever the case may be—for the price of two hundred quid had given the twins his address plus a description of a boy who worked for Mule so they could blame him for blabbing. The kid hadn't wanted to give his own name, but that was all right. So long as he kept his gob shut, George didn't care. It seemed he would, as he'd shaken all over and scooted off pretty sharpish after he'd snatched the offered money.

In the van, they sat outside Mule's two-bed semi, a nice house on the better side of Bracknell. He was a fool to shit on his own doorstep, selling where he lived, but some people never learnt to play by the rules. He was also a fool for doing it without permission, and he'd soon find out the hard way that playing nice was the better option. There would be no leeway. George intended to send out a message to the masses, one he hoped they'd listen to this time. They'd rounded up drug pushers in the past and put the word out about the rules around here, but it seemed some people still weren't listening. Knobs.

George glanced at Greg. "Which routine are we going with?"

Greg shrugged. "This is your gig, so you choose."

"We'll play at being buyers."

Greg chuffed out air. "The size of us two... Do you really think he'll believe that? We don't look like the usual skagheads."

George laughed. "All sorts take drugs, you know that. All we need is to get him to open the front door. The rest will be easy."

They left the van, George leading the way up the concrete garden path, thankful he'd handed out black beards for their disguises today. If he'd come here with a ginger one on, Mule might have recognised him from last night and let the cat out of the very big bag George was currently carrying in the form of his secret.

Greg moved to stand out of the way so he wouldn't be seen from any of Mule's windows. George knocked, standing close to the door for the same reason. The porch overhang shielded him from upstairs, and all Mule would hopefully see if he glanced through the living room window was a slice of George's side.

A shape appeared behind the glass stippled with what the designer must have felt were artistic splodges, then vanished just as quickly, as if the occupant had poked his head out of a doorway to see who stood there and decided whoever it was wasn't good. Impatient, George knocked again, unwilling to bend on this, unwilling to retreat and come back another time.

It was now or never, and if he had to break the glass to get in, he'd do it.

He bent to open the letterbox, greeted by that weird black furry stuff that kept draughts out. He parted it so he could speak through the gap he'd created. "Come on. For fuck's sake, man, I just want some gear." He stood upright, shifting his eyes across to Greg, and whispered, "He's cautious."

"Probably because of the police presence over the other side of the estate. Guilty people assume the worst. He must think we're the rozzers."

"In tracksuits?"

The shape appeared again, coming closer and closer, and the door opened a couple of inches, the chain on. No face filled the gap, but a gun did. The tattoo on the back of the hand, an eagle, meant the owner was their target. George was surprised, given Mule's name, that he hadn't gone with the picture of a donkey.

The sound of running water filtered out.

"No fucking me about," Mule grated in the type of voice that said he was trying too hard to sound tough. "How did you know where I live? Who sent you?"

George could handle this prick; he sounded scared, cagey. "I dunno what his name is, he didn't say. Some scruffy eejit outside the shops." He prepared himself to reel off the description of the kid who worked for Mule. "Short hair, blond. Camo puffa jacket. Skinny jeans. He had a mole on his nose as well as a load of freckles."

"Stupid little twat. I'll bloody kill him. You go to my usual spots in future. Never come here again after this, got it?"

"Yeah." That was the truth. George had no intention of returning.

"What do you want?"

"Got a party tonight, so a shit ton of weed and a few of baggies of coke. That should see us right. I've got five hundred quid, so whatever that will buy."

"Show me the money. Nothing gets done otherwise. I don't know you from Adam."

What a bell-end. George took the notes Greg handed over and flapped them in the gap.

"Who gave you that?" Mule asked. "I saw you take it off someone."

"Jesus, calm your tits. My brother."

"Wait there."

Like fuck.

Mule's shape walked towards natural light, a window at the back most likely, then it was gone. George handed the cash back to Greg and waited for Mule to return. He estimated when he was halfway down the hall. George kicked the door inwards, the chain flying free, and barged inside, Mule in the process of turning tail to run. George lunged for him, rugby tackling him to the laminate, a beautiful crunching sound proving Mule's nose had broken. He choked, probably on blood, and George grinned.

"I heard you've been a naughty boy," he said into Mule's ear, low and chilling, letting his heavy weight crush the bastard. "Selling where you're not allowed. The Brothers are here, and you're about to learn a very painful lesson."

"Oh God…"

"People always ask Him for help. Funny, that, because He never does. Maybe it's because He created people to be good and He's not into helping your sort."

George stood, yanking him up with him, and half dragged, half marched him out of the house. Someone opposite had come out for a nose, a fella in a shirt with a blue jumper draped over his shoulders, the sleeves in a knot at his puny chest.

Fucking ponce. He soon went indoors when George sent a glare his way and Greg mimed slitting his throat.

"Leave the front door open," George said. "Let him get ransacked. Someone's bound to gossip that he's been carted off, and people will want a freebie."

"Arsehole," Mule muttered.

"Is that meant to hurt my feelings?" George asked. "I've been called worse, and that didn't upset me either. Now shut your fucking cakehole and get in there."

Greg opened the rear door of the van, and George pushed Mule inside. He climbed in after him, pinned him on his front on the floor, and grabbed a cable tie from a nearby open toolbox, cuffing his wrists. The door closed, and Greg got in the driver's seat, screeching away from the kerb. George sat on the wheel arch, leaving Mule to turn himself over, impersonating a landed fish. Mule stared at him, squinting in thought, then shook his head. Blood coated his face, his nose skewed to one side.

"I bet that's minging," George said. "Your nose."

"Fuck you."

George tutted. "I don't think you're in a position to get lairy."

"What do you want? I left a fucking bath running, and my place will get flooded."

"And? That's the least of your worries. It's not like you're ever going back there, so stop getting your dick in a flap. Let me explain the situation so you're under no illusion as to why we've picked you up."

Mule seemed to have realised this wasn't any ordinary kidnapping. His face paled, and his body had lost the rigidity of anger, the shakes replacing any bravado he'd once had.

"We heard you might have killed two people last night," George said over the rumble of the engine. "Buyers of yours."

"Fuck off! That wasn't me, but I saw who did it." Mule coughed then gobbed bloodied spit on the floor.

George made a mental note to get their special crew in to clean the van, inside and out. "Did you? Shame I don't believe you."

"Who *are* you?"

George sighed. He hated it when people didn't pay attention. "Are you deaf? I've already told you back at your place."

Mule swallowed. "The Brothers?"

"Yes, sunshine, The Brothers."

Their work phone blared a tinny ringtone, and Greg held it out towards George.

He took it and glanced at the screen, wondering what Moon could want. "All right, mate?"

"Brickhouse has been shot."

Anger, immediate and hot, flooded George's system, begging Mad to come out and play. He had the urge to stomp on Mule's face and end him here and now but held it back. "You what?"

"Yeah. He didn't get a chance to tell me where he was before the call got cut off. He spoke fast, like he didn't have much time. Aster has been abducted from her flat, and he'd followed a van. As he went to fire at whoever took her, he was shot. I've sent Alien around to hers to see what's going on there. He's dealing with two squawking birds at the minute. My copper's in the process of finding out the general location of Brickhouse's phone, but as you can imagine, he's got to be careful, so it might take him a while."

"Didn't anyone ring the police after hearing a gunshot?"

"Not that my plod is aware, but he's keeping an ear out and will let me know so we can act accordingly. From what I could gather, there are two sites where shots were fired. Aster's and wherever Brickhouse is."

"Fuck."

"Where are you?" Moon asked.

"In the van. We've picked someone up. Another job that needed dealing with."

"Are you going to the warehouse?"

"Yeah, our quarry will need to stay there so we can find Aster and Brickhouse."

"My pig's also searching for Brickhouse's car, but if he's incapacitated and some other coppers find him, we're in the shit in more ways than one."

"What do you mean?"

"Someone else was shot. The abductor did it. At Aster's flat. He didn't say the name, but it's a woman. Brickhouse took her with him when he drove after the van that had Aster in it. He said she was still in his car, the shot woman, either dead or out for the count, so we really need to find it to hush this mess up. She could wake up and create merry hell. Attract attention."

"Shit."

"We'll keep each other posted. I don't have to tell you that if I lose Brickhouse, it'll be a sad day, and I'll be raging."

"I know, mate. Speak soon." George swiped the screen and got hold of Martin. "Look, I know you don't like getting involved in the shitty stuff, but I need you at the warehouse to babysit someone."

"I thought I was meant to be relieving Will outside that Steve bloke's house later."

"So did I, but things have changed. I'll get someone else on that. Bring drinks and something to eat. We don't have time to sort anything for you." He swiped the screen again and met Greg's eyes in the rearview mirror. "Things have gone a bit tits up, bruv."

"Tell me when we've dropped this gimp off."

George nodded and smiled at Mule, even though he didn't feel much like showing his pearly-whites. "Seems you've got a slight reprieve, my old son. Lucky you."

With Mule tied to the chair, Martin playing Xbox while looking after him, Greg drove towards Aster's flat, George munching sweets in the passenger seat. Janine was going to look at ANPR to find Brickhouse's car but couldn't do it right away as she was currently at the morgue speaking to the pathologist about the Bracknell kills. With the police side of things out of their hands, there was nothing they could do on that front until word came back.

Greg had an uneasy feeling. George wasn't his usual self, something about him was off, although Greg couldn't put his finger on it. If he was asked to explain it, he wouldn't be able to, so for now, he'd observe and try to work it out.

"This is a monumental fuck-up," George said. "How the chuff did she get abducted?"

Greg shook his head in wonder. "I don't know, because Brickhouse is shit-hot in what he does. Something must have gone wrong, he was ambushed."

"It frustrates the hell out of me, not knowing, but when we catch up with whoever did this…"

"I know. I feel the same. They've taken the piss out of us, not to mention the fact Aster must be crapping herself and Brickhouse might be dead." Greg swerved into a free parking space in Aster's road and got out, sensing George following.

Alien stood in front of the block of flats, a couple of women with him. "Thank God you're here. Explain to these two that we've got it under control and they don't need to involve the police." He frowned, looking George and Greg up and down. "What the fuck have you two got on?"

"Been on another job." Greg peeled his beard off and stared at the two gawping birds. "As you can see, it's me and George, so tell us your addresses, and we'll make sure a little payment gets delivered—providing you keep your traps shut."

The one with brown plaits nodded. "Okay, okay, it's just...this woman got shot, and some bloke dumped her in his car, and some *other* woman was put inside a van by another fella."

"Did you get the van's number plate?" Greg asked.

"It looked like a personal one. Spelled out P I Nort."

Handy. If it's real. The PI... Did Aster's old man hire a private detective to track her down? "Cheers. Our police officers are aware, do you understand?"

Brown Plaits nodded. "Yes."

191

"Did anyone else come out here before our friend arrived?" Greg gestured to Alien.

"No, just us. Everyone else will probably be at work. I'm between jobs, and my mate came round for the day." She flapped her hand at the blonde who had really bad extensions. That or she was having a shitty hair day.

"Right. If anyone you speak to round here mentions it, you tell them the twins know, got it?"

Brown Plaits nodded again. "Right. When will the money come? Only, I'm nearly out of electric on the prepayment meter, and we're gasping for a cup of tea."

George tutted and stepped forward, handing over twenty quid. "Get it topped up. Now piss off."

They scuttled off up the road, heading for the street where the shops were, glancing over their shoulders at them.

"Thank fuck they've gone," Alien muttered.

George grunted. "I'll message Janine and Moon about that number plate. P I Nort. What a knob. You'd think he'd use a falsie when out on a job like this."

"Could still be false," Greg said. Then to Alien, "Have you been up to Aster's flat to check it out?"

He nodded. "It was the first thing I did. That was when those two came and knocked on the door, asking me questions. No blood in the flat, just out here, and from the spatter pattern on the path, she was shot over there, not inside. Aster's flat door was open, so I assume someone paid them a visit and it all went pear-shaped, Brickhouse more interested in following than securing the flat. There's no CCTV, I looked, otherwise you could have got hold of your bloke at the council."

George got his phone out again, gritting his teeth. "I'll message him anyway in case the cameras are hidden. If they captured anything, we'll get a copy, then it needs erasing from the system in case someone's phoned the shooting in but they haven't come out here to see what's what."

"We'd best get going then," Alien said. "We don't want to be here if and when the police arrive."

Greg sighed, wishing he'd opened his mouth earlier and suggested Brickhouse took Aster to a safe house. Too bloody late now for hindsight to blab its gob off with recriminations.

They wandered back to the road.

"Who was the woman who got shot?" George mused.

"Probably a decoy," Alien said. "By sending a woman to Aster's door, it's less suspicious than a man. I'm confused as to why the door was even opened. Why Brickhouse allowed it. That isn't like him to drop the ball. Maybe Aster knew the visitor." He waved. "Anyway, I'm out of here."

"Yep." Greg walked round to the driver's side of their van and opened it. He got in, and while he waited for George to join him, the penny dropped. He stared, open-mouthed, at his twin who did his seat belt up. "Aster said she met two women last night and gave them her address..."

"Nah, it's too convenient for Aster to have approached those two specifically at The Baker's Dough. Is that what you're saying, that the bloke who drove onto the pavement set it all up so Aster would go up to them? She could have chosen anyone, there'd have been a few outside smoking. How would he know she'd choose them?"

"I know that, and it wasn't what I meant. What if that bloke was watching? What if he followed them when they went to The Roxy and The Angel, then he waited for the women to finish clubbing and tailed them home? Convinced one of them to call on Aster today? And before you say anything, it isn't a stretch. Hardly anyone knows where Aster lives, not even her old mates from where she worked before, she told us that, so it's a bit too obvious for someone to turn up at her flat today, *the day after* Aster told them where she lives."

"What did she say their names were?"

"Sarah and Kallie."

George got the phone out and sent a message. "I'm getting someone to go to The Baker's to keep an eye out. Hopefully, the one who wasn't shot will go there for a bevvy."

"Who are you sending?"

"Jimmy Riddle."

Greg smiled and drove away. "Makes sense. He's quick, and she won't outrun him." He wasn't sure what to do now, where to go. With no word from Moon or Janine yet, they were in limbo. He didn't want to go to the warehouse to sort Mule as they had to be on hand in case they were needed urgently. "We'll nip to The Angel, put some feelers out there. The Baker's is only a couple of streets away, so who knows, this Kallie might be a regular at Debbie's, too. Someone'll open their mouth if we flash the cash."

"They'd better, because with a shot woman in a car, Aster and Brickhouse in the wind, we need a break."

Greg turned the corner and stopped in front of the women on the corner. He got out and questioned them about a Sarah and Kallie, but no one knew who they were. Back in the van, he parked it round the back of The Angel so George could take his beard off and they could strip out of the clothes they'd put on over their suits.

It was one of the times they needed to be The Brothers so everyone knew they meant business.

Chapter Fifteen

Aster stared at the man in the lift. "Who the fuck are *you*?"

"Jesus, keep your hair on, love. If this is the thanks I get for helping someone, I won't bother in future. I thought you were meant to pay it forward, but it seems I was wrong. Talk about ungrateful."

Was this a trap? Was he just saying that to make her think he wasn't in on this? Wasn't working for Dad?

She studied him warily. "Excuse me if I wondered what a man was doing, dragging me into a lift," she said. "I mean, that's totally *normal* behaviour, isn't it."

Her sarcasm hung heavy between them, scratching at the air and her nerves.

He shrugged and jabbed the button for what she assumed was his floor. Thankful it wasn't the same one for the flat she'd hidden in years ago, Aster relaxed a bit.

Unless this is a ruse and Dad's waiting on another level. Shit.

"What the fuck was going on out there?" the man asked. "By the way, I'm Colin."

She ignored his question. "Do you know a Steve Huckstable?"

"Err, nope. Should I?"

He seemed genuine, but Aster trusted so few people, she wouldn't take what he'd said as the truth.

"Who's *he*?" Colin asked.

"My dad."

"Right. And does he have something to do with what happened out the front? Let's not dance around the issue. Someone got fucking *shot*." He took his phone out and poked at the screen.

Alarm pierced Aster. Was he going to ring Dad? "What are you doing?"

"What do *you* think? Phoning the police."

"Do phones work in lifts?"

He shrugged. "I'll give it a go anyway."

He didn't get the chance. The lift lurched to a stop, and the doors opened. Aster braced herself for seeing Dad, but only a woman and a baby in a buggy stood there. Was her father hiding out of sight, ready to pounce? Was Colin a good actor and really Dad's friend or just someone he'd roped in to help him out?

Cautious, her veins on fire from the rush of blood, Aster left the lift behind Colin who walked over to a floor-to-ceiling window that overlooked the front. Aster checked the landing. No one. The lift doors shut the occupants inside, and the sense of being in danger intensified now she was alone again with a stranger. And what if Dad shot the lady as she got out of the lift, thinking she was Aster? Would he kill the baby, too?

Oh God.

Colin stared down. "Oh, he's gone."

Aster went over and stared down, too. Brickhouse wasn't there, but his car was.

"What the fuck's that?" Colin pointed.

Aster's pulse went thready. What was she supposed to be looking at? "Where?"

"The back seat, side window of the red car."

Aster squinted. "Jesus Christ, is that a woman?" She knew damn well it was once she'd stared harder, and relief barrelled through her, tainted with a speck of fear in case Dad went out there and did some damage.

Sarah's face, shrouded in condensation from her breaths against the glass, showed her panic and desperation, her fingers pressed to the window, the sight like something out of a film. Two things warred inside Aster: resentment towards Sarah for her betrayal, and doing the right thing and helping her.

What would The Brothers tell me to do?

Get the fuck away from here and ignore Sarah, let them deal with her.

Could she do that, though? Despite Sarah doing what she had, did she deserve to die? The twins weren't going to let her go, she'd have to be punished.

If Aster had her phone, she could ring the twins, but she bloody well didn't, and she hadn't memorised their number either. Who even did that these days? Would phoning the police mess the whole operation up? Yes. Aster's mind ticked over and provided a solution, one that would appease Colin and keep things under wraps at the same time.

"Look," she said. "There's this copper who will help. Her name's Janine Sheldon. She works at the Cardigan nick. Phone and ask for her."

Colin stabbed at his screen and Googled the correct police station. He found a link to the number and pressed it. At least now she knew he was genuine.

"Put it on speaker," Aster said.

Colin did that, and a man answered, saying he was a sergeant.

"Can I speak to Janine Sheldon?" Colin asked.

"What's this regarding?"

Colin glanced at Aster who shook her head: *Don't tell him anything.*

"I'd rather not say. I need to speak to her, only her. It's really urgent. Proper urgent."

A sigh. "I'll see where she is. Hold the line."

Aster and Colin held eye contact as the seconds ticked by, their fears palpable, although Aster's were for different reasons to what she imagined Colin's were. He'd be scared because a man had got shot and a woman begged for someone, anyone, to let her out of that car.

"Still there, sir?" the copper asked.

Colin jumped. "Um, yeah."

"You got lucky. She's just walked into the station. I'll patch you through."

A rustle came over the line, and breathing, as if someone walked while on the phone. "DI Janine Sheldon. Who am I speaking to, please?"

Aster took over. "I'm being helped by The Brothers."

"Oh. Right. Hang on, I need to go somewhere quiet." More heavy breathing. A door closed. "Okay, what's the matter?"

"I haven't got my phone, and I need to get hold of them. Tell them Aster's—"

Another gunshot, so loud, so *there*, and Colin collapsed, his phone dropping and skittering across the floor. Aster shouted out in shock and spun around. Dad stood there, he must have come up the stairs, not in the lift, and he mimed zipping his lips. He walked over to Colin's phone, the gun trained on Aster, and reached down and cut the call.

The stupid prat hasn't got gloves on.

If his fingerprint was the way he'd be caught for this, Aster would be happy. Whatever happened now, at least he'd left some evidence behind.

"Get in the lift, Albie," he said and put the phone in his pocket. "You've caused enough trouble for one day."

She backed towards it, no intention of going inside. A glance at Colin, and she almost vomited. One side of his face had been blown off. Blood and gore spattered the window, and through the specks, she made out the sky, the clouds, the tops of the houses opposite. Would that be the last time she saw the outside? What if Dad shot her next? And why the fuck hadn't anyone come out of their flats on this level, any bloody level, to see what had happened? Did a gunshot mean people cowered inside? Wouldn't someone have phoned the police?

At the last second, she dashed for the stairs, her heart pounding, everything in slow motion. Each step seemed to take forever to navigate, but she made it down to the elbow landing without getting shot. On she went, down to the next level, then down again, no sign of Dad following her. She reached the fourth floor, and the lift dinged, a warning for her to get a move on; it could be him. She gripped the handrail and swung herself round to the next set of steps, but a hand clutching her hair from behind stopped her short. She grunted through the pain of her roots being yanked, then she was dragged into the lift, whipped round so she stared at the mirror at the back. She caught a glimpse of Dad in the reflection, the doors closing, the gun aimed at her head. If he shot her, would she see her face explode? Or would she be dead before that happened?

The lift's descent had her stomach rolling.

"You should have known you wouldn't be able to get away from me for good," Dad said, coming closer, butting the end of the gun to her temple.

Aster closed her eyes. She couldn't stand to look at his reflection anymore. He grabbed one of her wrists and pressed his chest to her back, his breathing loud in her ear.

"Now then, we're going to the flat. No screaming. No fuss. Just do as you're bloody told. All I want is a chat, to catch up after all these years."

Aster laughed with nerves. "What, and then you'll let me go? Do you think I'm stupid?"

"Far from it. You've been clever in hiding yourself for a long time, but not quite clever enough."

The lift *dinged*. She spun round, wrenching her wrist from his hold, ready to push him when the doors opened and run for her life, but he shoved the end of the gun in her mouth and curled his finger around the trigger.

"Try me," he said.

Aster's eyes fuzzed with tears. She'd lost her freedom. She'd be stuck with him again. He'd force her back through little windows. Chain her up in the house.

"Are you going to behave?" Dad stuck his foot back to stop the doors closing.

Aster nodded.

"Good boy."

The flat looked exactly the same. Dad must have taken it over since…since all that shit had happened back then. The smell, though, that was different. Multiple cleaning products, their scents mixed together, stale but still recognisable. Dad shoved her in the back, down the hallway and into the spare bedroom. What was he going to do, hold her captive in there? Keep on and on at her for days until she agreed to go home and do what he wanted? A part of her worried he still had the ability to wear her down, but a bigger part rebelled against it. She hadn't run away, found a new life, only for him to snatch it from her. She wouldn't let him.

She gasped in shock and relief. Brickhouse lay on the single bed, his wrists tied in front of him, his ankles bound by rope, his eyes closed. His chest rose and fell in a steady rhythm — thank God he wasn't dead.

"What did you do, drag him indoors?" She had to know if there was an accomplice, someone else Dad had lured into his sick world.

"It took me a while because he's so fucking heavy, but yeah." He snatched her wrist again, a warning for her not to try and run, digging his nails into her skin.

"Liar," Brickhouse said, eyes still shut. "You had a gun to my head. You said if I didn't go with you, you'd kill Aster."

Dad gritted his teeth. "I've fucking *told* you, pal, it's *Albie*."

Aster fought back tears; the gun was still pointed at her, so she didn't dare bolt. Not a second time. Dad's patience wouldn't stretch that far. And although Brickhouse was tied up, she was safer with him here. Somehow, they'd get away. Tell The Brothers where they were. Unless Dad had searched Brickhouse, there had to be a phone in the big man's pocket. Shit, what if it rang and Dad took it away?

Brickhouse had done his job to the letter, protecting her, doing as he'd been told so he could at least be with her here. She couldn't get over it and, uncharitably, thought he should have got up and run once he'd come round from being shot so Aster could be rescued, not stuck in this flat with a fucking maniac. Or had Dad been out the front at that point, ready to shoot him?

"On your knees, Albie," Dad said.

She glanced at Brickhouse who nodded imperceptibly. Although her instincts screamed at her to run, to ignore both of their instructions, she obeyed. Dad grabbed a length of rope, tucked the gun in his waistband, and secured her wrists. He went behind her to tie her ankles then pushed her forward so she landed face-first on the floor. A flash of pain burst in her cheek.

"There was no need for that," Brickhouse said.

Dad laughed. "Like I give a fuck about your opinion." He stared at Aster. "Now then, I'm going to be nice and let you two have a little chat, but after that, you'll be gagged. There's no point in screaming or shouting, next door is empty. The bird in the third flat is on holiday, and the fella in the fourth is at work. As for the others, they're too far away to hear jack shit. You've got an hour, then the conversion can begin."

Conversion?

Dad bent down and gripped Aster beneath the armpits, dragging her to the bed and propping her spine against it. She couldn't see Brickhouse behind her but sensed his presence, and that was enough to calm her.

Dad walked out, slammed the door, and the thud of his footsteps had Aster shaking.

"What the fuck?" Brickhouse said. "I thought you'd got away."

"I did." She explained about Colin.

"He *shot* him? Jesus Christ…"

Another slam. The front door?

Brickhouse sighed. "I bet he's gone to get the body. He'll be lucky if someone hasn't found Colin and phoned the police."

"Colin rang Janine. She can trace who the phone belongs to, can't she? She'll tell George and Greg where Colin lives, won't she?"

"Yep, and someone else is bound to have phoned the coppers, but in the meantime, we're stuck here with that piece of shit."

"Sarah's outside in your car," she said. "Do you think she'll tell the police what happened? She was scared of that man who took me. He told her he'd hurt her family if she didn't do what he wanted. What if she clams up and doesn't say anything? What if my Dad kills us?"

"He won't. He's a bit fucking thick if he doesn't realise what he's done."

Aster's mind was so full of questions and swirling panic that she was confused. "What do you mean?"

"He left us together. Without gags."

"So?"

"We've got teeth, haven't we?"

It took a moment for Aster's brain to clear, to catch up, and she smiled. "Who's biting the knots first then, me or you?"

Leaving the flat with Brickhouse's leg giving him gyp slowed them down. Aware of how much time had passed since Dad had walked out, how he might be in the lift now with a dead Colin, Aster took the keys Brickhouse handed to her and ran across to his car. She clicked the locks open and dived into the back seat with Sarah.

"Can you drive?" Aster asked her.

"Yes."

Brickhouse lumbered to the front passenger side and got in, letting out a grunt of pain.

Aster handed Sarah the keys. "Hurry up, for fuck's sake."

"But I've been shot." Sarah winced and carefully opened the door.

"Where?" Brickhouse asked.

"In the arm."

"This is an automatic, and you can drive with one hand."

Sarah got out and walked around to the driver's side, her movements lethargic. She got in, inserted the key, and Brickhouse put the gearstick in DRIVE. She peeled out of the parking space, her breathing heavy, and Aster glanced at the high-rise.

Dad stared from the living room window of the flat, his face a mask of anger.

"Shit, he's clocked us," Aster said.

"Doesn't matter." Brickhouse gritted his teeth. "He'll be dealt with now we know the address." He turned to Sarah. "Have you got a phone? He took mine."

"In my bag." Sarah coasted right at the end of the street.

"So why the fuck didn't you phone the police then?" Brickhouse barked.

"That man…what he said. I was too scared to."

The handbag strap hung across Sarah's body, and Brickhouse opened the front flap and ferreted inside. He took her phone out.

"PIN?" he asked.

"Six, eight, nine, one."

Aster breathed a sigh of relief. They were out of the woods for now, but if Dad was as savvy as she thought, he'd leave Colin in the flat and hide somewhere else, then come back to find her again when some time had passed. If The Brothers didn't locate him, Aster would have to move on, again, and start a new life, worrying he'd track her down even if she left London.

"Boss, it's me," Brickhouse said into the phone. "Meet us at the clinic. Tell The Brothers to go to this address but to watch out for the police." He reeled it off, cut the call, and prodded the screen, then held it up for Sarah to see. "Follow the route."

He'd accessed Google, and a blue line lit up.

"What's the clinic?" Aster asked.

"Two people with bullets in them? We can't exactly go to an NHS hospital without being asked questions, can we," he said. "My boss' people will fix it." He paused, then ground out, "And the twins will fix *him*."

He meant Dad.

"But he'll go off somewhere," Aster said. "He's not stupid enough to stay in the flat."

Sarah swerved to miss some old dear crossing the road. "What the fucking hell is going on here? All I was told was your dad wanted to see you, that you had unfinished business. I didn't expect to be caught up in this crap."

"Well, you are," Brickhouse said. "And you'd better hope The Brothers don't deal with *you*, too."

Chapter Sixteen

*K*aren fitted in the big burgundy suitcase. Just. Dad had forced Albie to put her in there, and the slip-slide of blood on his hands as he'd touched her had been revolting, incriminating. It was drying now, drawing his skin tight, and he wanted to run and get it off. Dad had cleaned his own hands. Blood had spattered onto his face and dotted his white T-shirt, one Karen had washed and ironed last week, and he'd scrubbed his cheeks and put on a clean top, shoving the dirty one into the washing machine. He zipped the case up, lugging it off the sofa and dumping it on the carpet. Idly, Albie wondered if any blood would seep through.

"Go and get in the shower," Dad said, his expression so rigid, his hands balled at his sides, like he was trying to contain whatever temper he had left.

Albie wasn't surprised Dad still had that evil fire raging inside him. The murder—oh God, it was murder—wouldn't have erased his anger. It was always on a constant simmer, waiting to be unleashed at any given moment. He'd use it as a whip to strike Albie with in a minute if he didn't do as he was told.

"I... What are you going to do with her?"

"You'll see. Get some clean clothes on after. Take a black bag up with you to put your dirty stuff in. You're bound to have got blood on them. We can't risk anyone seeing that, understand?"

Albie understood all right. Dad expected him to help cover this up. If they got caught, he'd probably blame Albie for it. Dad had always said he would never go in the nick, he'd do whatever it took to go into hiding, and pinning it all on his son would be the easy way to go.

Albie left the room, stepping over the puddle of blood in the hallway that had seeped out of Karen's

216

head while Dad had rushed upstairs for the suitcase. Albie wished all that scarlet wasn't there and that Karen was still alive. That they were just finishing up dinner, getting ready to eat the apple crumble she'd popped into the oven around five o'clock. In the kitchen, he glanced at the cooker. Used a tea towel to cover his hand so he could turn the temperature dial down to zero—the less places that had blood transferred the better. He opened the door to let the heat out. The crumble was well and truly done, some parts of the topping verging on burnt.

He got a black bag from the cupboard beneath the sink, hopped over the blood again, and rushed upstairs. He got in the shower with his clothes on and peeled them off under the spray, his tears meshing with the water, a lump in his throat, sobs building. A second mother had been stolen from him, and there was nothing left for him now. He should take his stash of money, nick Karen's flat keys from the hiding place she'd mentioned. He swallowed the glut of emotion that barged into him at the thought of her trusting him enough to tell him where the key was. Maybe it was so if Dad ever went too far with Albie, he'd have somewhere to go. Yes, he'd go to her place for a bit. All right, Dad might come round, he'd probably guess where he'd gone, but Albie could ignore the door. Dad wouldn't chance breaking in because of the neighbours and, once Albie had formulated a plan, he could go elsewhere. Where, he had no clue, so he'd take this one minute at a time. Deal with one thing at a time.

For now, he'd have to play along with Dad until he could escape.

He reached out of the bath for the black bag, wrung his soaked clothes out and dropped them inside, tossing the bag onto the floor. The rage Dad had shown was so intense, it was like he'd morphed into a monster, there was no other word for it. Had his temper frayed like that with Mum? Had he killed her, too, like Albie suspected and Dad had all but confirmed when he'd said what the high price was? Where had he done it? Downstairs when Albie had been asleep? Or at the office? Dad had told everyone she'd fucked off with another man, so was that why no one had come round to see where she was? Why no one cared that she'd been here one minute, gone the next? Even his grandparents hadn't bothered asking questions, not that Albie remembered anyway. Didn't they care that she'd just up and left?

Karen had told him about her parents, that they'd had her when they were older and were dead now. She'd said her flat was hers outright, her father had sold his business and given her enough to buy it, and she'd told Dad when he'd grumbled about it that as it was her first home, she'd keep it, it had sentimental value. It was obvious now that she'd done it in case she needed somewhere to go, but surely when her wages stopped going in and the bills weren't paid, someone would get suspicious. When she didn't turn up for work, her boss might get worried.

What if her colleagues came to the flat to see if she was in when Albie was there?

This was all too much for a kid to deal with, but he'd have to.

My whole life has been too much to deal with.

He got out of the shower and dressed in his bedroom. Took the black bag downstairs and put it on the floor, away from the worst of the blood. The front door stood open, and the suitcase was on the step. Albie's guts churned at the thought of Karen squashed inside it, and it went over even more at the sound of Dad talking to someone. Who the hell was it? Had he phoned for Muttley to come round? Dad now had blue overalls on. Gloves. Did that mean he'd wiped the suitcase of fingerprints and didn't want to transfer more? He looked bulky where his other clothes were underneath. Lumpy. Odd.

"Yeah, just a couple of days," Dad said. "A little break by the sea."

"Bloody big suitcase for a couple of days," the next-door-but-one neighbour called out. Mrs Greaves. Old. She always came out to catch neighbours for a chat.

"There's my boy, too," Dad said. "He likes to take everything but the kitchen sink, hence the big case."

"Kids these days, eh? Mind you, I've seen you using that case at night a lot, yet you can't always be going away because you're back by the morning."

God, she must be talking about when Dad forced Albie inside it before they went to the office.

"You know what curiosity did to the cat, don't you?" Dad said.

"I do." Mrs Greaves sounded unfazed. "What about your wife?"

Dad chuckled. "Oh, I'm not married, and she's certainly not my wife. Dunno what gave you that impression."

"She told me you were married."

"Maybe she did that so if someone came round asking questions, people would tell them she was with me."

Albie frowned. Dad had instructed Karen to tell people they were married. Why was he lying?

"She's my sister," Dad went on. "She's gone back home now. Came to stay while she got over her divorce and the house sale went through. Her ex was being a *pest and holding up proceedings, which is why she was here for so long."*

He's such a good liar.

"Ah, poor love," Mrs Greaves said.

"Yeah, but she's on the up now."

"That's nice to hear. Anyway, I must get in."

Albie shut his eyes and let out a long breath at the sound of her front door closing. The clomp of Dad coming back to the front door had him snapping them open again.

"Fucking nosy bitch," Dad muttered. "I thought she'd never fuck off. I didn't want her seeing me struggling with the case. Sodding heavy. Stay away from the mess. I don't want you getting dirty again. I'll just put this bitch in the boot. Go and pack a bag for both of us, enough for two nights. I need to make good on the cover story I just gave her along the road."

Dad pulled the door to. He'd been such a prat leaving it open with the hallway light on. Anyone could have looked in and seen all that blood. Was he that confident in himself that he hadn't stopped to think about that?

Albie went upstairs and packed more than two days' worth of clothes, but only for himself. He stuffed his savings envelope in the bottom of the bag, beneath his things, then sat on his bed until the shower

221

switched on, Dad's clonking feet loud as he stepped into the bath. Quickly, Albie ran into the main bedroom and slowly opened the drawer beneath the divan bed on Karen's side. Right at the back, in a ring box, was the key to the flat. He checked it was inside, and a piece of paper caught his eye. It was rolled up tiny and tight, and he unfurled it. She'd written down the address, even though she'd already told him what it was. Grateful for her thoughtfulness, he tucked the box in his bag and went downstairs.

He gave the blood one last look, picked up the bag of wet clothes to dump on the way, said a silent sorry to Karen, then left the house, running off into the night.

Moonlight came through Karen's kitchen window, giving the room a creepy glow. She had food staples in the cupboards, stuff that wouldn't go off for ages. Pasta, rice, tins, and UHT milk cartons. It was as if she'd stocked up to use this as a bolthole. How long had she been planning her escape? It had to be a while, considering how much stuff was here. Had she ever thought to take Albie with her? Or had her comment about him being hers been a sign, her saying if he was hers, she could have snatched him away without *repercussions? What did that matter anyway, he was sixteen and could go where he liked. Maybe she hadn't thought of that. And maybe she hadn't been thinking about Albie at all, her mind on getting herself to freedom taking up all of her thoughts. No, that wasn't true. She'd mouthed* COME WITH ME. *She'd wanted him with her.*

He reckoned, if no one came round demanding that he leave, he could eke the food out for a couple of months, just topping it up a bit when he ran out of things. He'd live here quietly, so the neighbours thought no one was in, and at night he wouldn't put any lights on. He wouldn't go to school—it was the summer holidays soon anyway. He'd hide here until the heat had died down, then move on. Where, he didn't know, but one thing was for sure, he'd never go back to Dad.

Albie had at least two days where his father wouldn't come round. He'd be away, dumping the body and making out he was having that little holiday. And anyway, would he even come here? Wouldn't him being seen by someone put him at risk if the police started asking questions? Albie reminded himself that if Karen's boss got worried and put a string of events in motion, he'd have to leave here sooner.

He sat on the leather sofa in the living room, the chill of it cooling his hot body. He was dying to see what everything looked like in the light, but that would have to wait until the morning. The moon wasn't on this side of the building, everything shrouded in gloom. He went to the window and pulled one of the closed curtains across an inch or two, peering into the street. This flat was on the third floor of a tall block, three blocks altogether, houses tagged on either end. Opposite, a row of terraced homes stretched both ways, the street a long one—so long he couldn't see the entrances from here as the road dipped downhill and bent round corners slightly.

He returned to the sofa and itched to switch the telly on. That would be okay, wouldn't it? The curtains were thick, the lined sort, and surely no one would take any notice if the light from it seeped around them. Karen had said she didn't speak to any neighbours, so no one would know whether it was her in here or not.

He gave in, surprised at the time already. The ten o'clock news was on. He flicked over to a film, although he didn't see the images on the screen nor hear what was being said. What he did see was Karen being battered with the hot iron, and what he did hear was her mad noises then silence.

Tears fell, and the enormity of what he'd been through struck Albie fiercely.

He'd been an accessory to murder.

A week had gone by, and no one had called round. He'd got braver, putting the lamp on in the living room in the evenings, although he'd covered it with one of Karen's woolly scarves to mute the glow. It was so nice to be alone, no Dad on his case, no jobs with Muttley.

Had Dad been caught for the murder? Was that why he hadn't been here? At first, Albie had worried Dad would report him missing but then had talked himself out of that scenario. Dad wouldn't want the police in the house. He'd have undoubtedly cleaned up the blood by now but wouldn't want to risk leaving a spot or two that an eagle-eyed copper would notice. If the school had rung about Albie's absence, he'd likely spout that Albie was sixteen and could do what he liked, maybe even going as far as to say his son had found somewhere else to live, they'd parted ways.

What about Mrs Greaves? She'd already assumed Karen was Dad's wife. What if she'd been spying that night and had seen Albie running up the road, then Dad getting into the car and driving away?

The only thing Albie missed about being at home was knowing what was going on. The not knowing was doing his head in. Oh, and Karen, he missed her all right. She had photo albums in her bedside cabinet, and he'd looked at them just to be closer to her. In them, she'd been younger, on holiday with friends, smiling as if her future was bright, not the bleakness she'd entered when she'd moved in with Dad and Albie. He'd talked to her, as if she were really there, telling her his fears, asking her to give him a sign to let him know it would be okay to stay here forever. That wasn't going to happen, the food would run out eventually, even though he ate sparingly, and if she had any savings, it would deplete with the bills going out.

He'd rifled through her wardrobe and taken out some clothes that caught his eye, and for the first time since he'd played dress-up with Mum, he'd put on women's clothes and shoes and even played about with applying makeup. It comforted him, that feeling he got, as if the freedom to be himself at last had wrapped him in a big fluffy cloud. He'd spent the whole week so far living as a girl, and apart from the obvious worry about someone finding him here, all was right in his world.

This had been a time of healing, a time of discovery. He'd never heal completely, that was true, but he'd found a way to put a plaster over the gaping wound. If he became someone else, the person inside, he could pretend Albie had never existed. Maybe he could convince himself that he'd never been a boy, had never lost his mother and Karen, and that his father wasn't a murdering bastard.

That would be a fool's errand, though. Dad would keep looking for him, Albie was certain of that. He'd never rest until he'd caught up with him. Surely he'd see, given time, when the police didn't knock on his door, that Albie was going to keep their secrets hidden. Why would Albie ever tell a copper everything? He'd be done for breaking and entering, for his part in handling stolen goods, for standing by while Dad had killed Karen, then he'd stuffed her in that bloody suitcase, knowing her body would be taken somewhere and left to rot.

God, what if her body was found? What if there was some link in that suitcase or on the body that would send the police to Dad's? What if it was pictured on the news and Mrs Greaves recognised it? The bloody thing was distinctive with those cream corner caps.

He sat at the table in the kitchen and sobbed into his hands. His life had been a difficult one, so many ups and downs, tragedies, no way out for years, and it had taken the death of his second mother in order for him to grow a pair and run. If only Karen hadn't stood up for herself that night. If only she'd stayed quiet until the next day, then packed her things and left. She'd still be alive, here, and Albie would have come to live with her. They'd have been happy, wouldn't they?

He'd never know. Life had thrown up this new path he was now on, and he had no choice but to walk it. One foot in front of the other, on and on and on until he finally found himself somewhere he could be safe.

A knock on the door had him jumping, and he sat there, breathing heavily, his chest tight and his heart beating too fast. He swallowed, fear creeping up his windpipe, a fluttering setting up home below his Adam's apple that was just beginning to show. The knock came again and, quietly, he got up and tiptoed down the hallway towards the door, thankful for no glass, just a peephole.

He stared through it.

A man stood on the other side. Suit jacket and tie, a white shirt. He ran a hand through his swept-back blond hair and frowned. Knocked again. He stepped back, a doctor's bag in hand, and Albie relaxed a bit. It wasn't a copper.

Brave, Albie drew the bolts across, leaving the chain on, and opened the door. He had a dress and makeup on, but that was the least of his worries. The man stared at him for a moment, clearly stunned by what he was seeing, then he composed his features and smiled.

"Err, is Karen in?"

Albie shook his head. "Nah, she's gone on holiday."

"When was this?"

"Last week. I'm looking after her flat for her."

"Oh. Right. It's just I've been to the address we had on file for her, and the man there said she'd be here, that they'd split up."

He must have gone to Dad's.

Albie kept the fear tucked inside. "Yeah, that's why she's gone away. To clear her head and whatever." Had he sounded plausible? "Who are you anyway?"

"I'm from her work. We were a bit concerned because she hasn't been in, hasn't even phoned to let us know anything."

"She was cut up." Albie hid a wince; Dad might well have cut her up to dispose of her body. "Said she wanted to be spontaneous and just bugger off. Do something for herself for once."

"I see. Rather annoying of her. She could have let us know. Do you know when she'll be back?"

229

"Next month. She's gone on one of them cruises."

"And do you mind me asking who you are?"

Albie's stomach flipped. "I'm her cousin's son."

"Hmm. I didn't think she had any family left after her parents died."

"Well, she does, because otherwise, what am I doing here? I'm not Scotch mist." Mum had said that once, and it felt weird coming out of Albie's mouth, weird to steal a dead woman's words. "Look, the best I can do is let her know you came round, although it's been a bit spotty getting hold of her. No idea if they have internet on ships."

"Thank you, I appreciate that. Can you ask her to contact work? She's left us in an awful bind."

"Yep."

Albie closed the door and leant on it. He could only hope that had gone as well as he thought. He'd soon know if there was another knock on the door later and the police stood there.

Albie had no intention of opening the door then.

Chapter Seventeen

Steve punched the wall in the flat's living room. That fucking bastard son of his had got away again. There was no point in cursing himself, it wouldn't change anything, but he did it anyway. He'd thought he was so clever, leaving those two together, thinking Albie wouldn't hop out of the flat to get help for the big bloke. He hadn't considered them getting free and walking out together, their ankles and wrists free of rope. He'd been so caught up in the fear of that fella's body being discovered upstairs that he'd just wanted to get up there and collect him.

He'd planned, if people were on the landing, to say he'd heard a gunshot and had come to help. Thankfully, no one had been there, the majority of residents probably at work, so he'd dragged him into the lift and then draped him over his shoulder once they'd got to Steve's floor. Inside, he'd dumped the body on the sofa, then checked the landing to see if any blood had dripped. A couple of spots, so he'd wiped them with the sleeve of his jacket, then went back into the flat.

The spare bedroom door had been closed, and he'd pressed his ear to it, wanting to catch any conversation. The silence hadn't made sense, he'd expected them to be whispering, planning their escape, something he'd *wanted* them to do so that when Albie realised he *wasn't* escaping, the pain of that revelation would cut deep.

Finding the room empty had sent Steve into panic mode. The bastards had gone, and he'd rushed into the living room and nosed out of the window. The sight of Albie staring up at him as the red car had driven away scoured Steve's gut with a heavy dose of nausea. But that look, that expression—fear. Albie was still scared of him, and Steve could work with that. Play on it when he next set eyes on his son.

He turned and studied the dead fella on the sofa. Steve shouldn't have shot him, he should have forced him and Albie into the flat, and Steve's mate, the one who did gay conversions, would have given him advice on what to do with him, likely a quick strangle, the body dumped in the woods, and the worry of the dead bloke phoning the police would have been over. Now there was blood, evidence, and the police would be here soon, they had to be.

Steve pulled the man's phone out of his pocket. He switched it off like he had with the big fella's, paranoid at first that the police could locate it to this specific flat, but he remembered something he'd watched on the telly once, that they might not be able to pinpoint its location exactly because of mast ranges or whatever it was called. The general vicinity would show up, but that didn't matter, Colin lived in this block, so it was a given his phone would be here. The big man's would be a worry, though.

Steve took that one out of his pocket and wiped both over with his sleeves, keeping his hands beneath the material, then lobbed the mobiles out of the window. He shut the curtains, thinking about what to do next. He had a corpse to get rid of, but that could come later, much later, say in a couple of days once the police had been and gone. Because they *would* come. He was surprised they hadn't arrived already. Who the fuck didn't ring in the sound of gunshots? Or were they that strapped for officers, they hadn't been able to send anyone yet?

Whatever, he needed to leave.

He had blood on him from carrying the body. In the bathroom, he turned his jacket inside out then washed his hands and face. With no alternative—should the pigs come knocking, he didn't want to pretend at the front door that he hadn't heard anything, he was too panicked to act innocent—he walked out, hoping the fella didn't smell too badly by the time he came back, or before that, some nosy prick calling the police to report a nasty whiff. He avoided the lift, taking the stairs, and on the ground floor in the foyer, he scooted past a huddle of people who'd finally come out to see what had been going on.

A woman holding a squirming toddler appealed to the group. "Has anyone else phoned the police besides me?"

"I did," an elderly man said. "You'd think, with both of us doing it, they'd be here by now."

"Maybe they're waiting for one of them armed response units," Steve said on his way to the main door. "You're all risking it, hanging around. The gunman might still be here."

"Yet *you're* here," the old man sniped.

"Not for long."

Steve left the building, walking casually to his car so it didn't look like he had anything to hide. He'd been stupid talking to that lot but hadn't been able to help himself. At first, it had been an attempt to appear normal, that he wasn't the man everyone should be afraid of, but he'd gone over the top with the gunman comment. More words meant there was a bigger chance they'd remember his face.

I should have just kept my gob shut.

In his car, he gunned the engine to the sound of sirens, which sounded too close for comfort.

They took their fucking time.

He drove away and, just as he passed a few houses on the left, blue lights in the distance flashed in his rearview mirror. His stomach muscles went a bit haywire—what if the police followed him?—but he drove on regardless.

Luck was on his side. He navigated the corner and headed in the direction of The Glass Shard, a pub Norton spent time in when he wasn't working. Steve wanted to have words with him, like how he'd bolted soon after he'd shot the big bloke and that girl he'd recruited, leaving Steve in the lurch.

What a fucking liberty.

Norton sat in the pub, his nerves frazzled. Never in his time as a private investigator had he come into contact with someone so nasty. Steve had said Albie needed to be brought home, and that was supposed to be the end of it. But things had escalated. Norton had felt forced into recruiting that blonde woman, Sarah, into helping him lure Albie out of his flat. She'd been wary at first, until he'd mentioned hurting her family, then he'd produced the five hundred quid. Her eyes had lit up, chasing the fear of his threat away. Some people were terrible, weren't they, in what they were prepared to do for a few banknotes.

Himself included, if he were honest. Being a PI could be considered a sneaky profession if you thought about it. Lurking in bushes or behind walls, spying on people through binoculars and taking pictures of them with a long-range lens, catching them in whatever acts his clients had accused them of. It was usually men or women cheating on their partners, plus the odd missing person's case, which was what Steve had sold as his story to begin with: a man desperate to find his lad.

Now look. Steve had given Norton a gun 'in case things get hairy', and Norton had panicked, shooting Sarah. He'd shit himself and stuffed Albie into his van, then driven to the destination. It had gone even more wrong there, Norton shooting the massive man who'd followed in a red car. Albie had gone inside, so Norton had delivered him as promised, so he'd hightailed it out of there, determined to cut ties with Steve. But the thing was, Steve would know Norton had possibly killed two people, and he'd more than likely hold that over his head for the rest of his life.

Shit.

Norton supped some more of his pint, anxious about what to do next. Leave his wife and skip town? Go and live with his ageing mother on the Isle of Wight? She had a double-wide caravan there, it'd easily accommodate the pair of them, and if he got a job, he could keep out of her way so it wouldn't seem like he'd ruined her solitary retirement. She was a tad funny about having guests and would moan like buggery if he turned up, but what else could he do?

He supposed there was his old man in France, although they didn't get along. Norton could get a Tube to the Channel Tunnel terminal and fuck off abroad, using one of his fake IDs that he had for PI work. It had to be better than sticking around here, didn't it? In no time, he'd be wanted for murder; Steve was bound to grass him up if he got caught. Staying in London was a big fat no.

Head down, he rose, preparing to leave, when a hand gripped his upper arm. He stared up at two identical people, blond beards and eyebrows, beanie hats, grey tracksuits covering bulky bodies, and his legs almost went from under him.

"All right, my old son?" one of them said. "We'd like a word with you."

In his car, Steve sat outside The Glass Shard and watched Norton come out with two men. Were they the police? Those undercover sorts? Had to be, what with the tracksuits. Then again, they carted him towards a small van with a sign that said BETTY'S CAKES on the side, and they shoved him in the back, one of them getting in with him.

There were only two people Steve knew who were twins and happened to be that size, although as far as he knew, The Brothers didn't have beards and weren't blond. What would they want with Norton, though, and how had they known where he was?

It was something to be answered on another day, because Steve had more pressing things on his mind. Like whether Norton would blab about who he currently worked for.

"Fucking gimp," he muttered and contemplated following the van now it was driving off, but that would be pushing his luck. He couldn't afford to mess with those two, if that's who they were.

Now then, where could he go? The flat was out of bounds, obviously, and it was a risk and a half to go to the house, but his passport was there. He reckoned, if he stayed away for a couple of months, Spain say, he could come back and begin his search for Albie again. He'd waited all these years, so what was another eight weeks?

Nothing.

George marched the man into the warehouse, Greg behind him.

Martin turned from his position on the sofa, paused his game, and sighed. "*Another* one?"

"Yeah," George said.

Janine had helped them out with the location of the PI's van. The number plate, P I NORT, had come up on ANPR, and she'd given him the exact location of The Glass Shard, where a street camera had picked it up. There was heavy CCTV in that area on account of it being rough as arseholes, and they'd entered the pub, discreetly asking if anyone knew of someone who was a private detective going by the name of Nort.

"You mean Norton," the landlord had said. "Yeah, it's that fella over there, crying into his pint."

Now, George smiled. They still had Steve to find, but first, he wanted to talk to Brickhouse and Aster, see if they knew anything that could locate the bastard man.

Greg helped him to strap a whimpering Norton to the rack.

"Look, shut up, will you?" George said. "I've got one nerve left, and you're on it."

"I-I didn't know it w-would go this f-far."

"You had a gun and used it—your choice. You shot a woman and one of my mates. What did you expect would happen, you could walk off into the sunset?"

"It all w-went wrong. I p-panicked."

"Twat," George said. "Tell me where Steve's likely to be if he isn't at home or at the flat."

"He's got an office."

"Where?"

Norton closed his eyes. "I don't k-know."

George punched him in the dick. "Are you sure?"

Eyes wide and watering, Norton nodded. "I swear, I don't know."

241

George believed him. It was okay, Janine could track any properties Steve owned or rented. He messaged Moon to help with that, too, and, about to put the phone in his pocket, he stopped at the sound of it ringing.

"Fuck me sideways," he muttered at the unknown number and swiped to answer.

Ida stood at her living room window behind the obscurity of her nets and smiled. "He's back."

"When did he arrive?" one of the twins asked.

"He's just pulled up now in that SUV thing. It looks like your man in the car is trying to phone you."

"Yep, I've got call waiting bleeping in my ruddy ear."

"Shall I go out there and distract him?"

"You could do, but any sign of danger, and you go inside."

Ida wasn't daft, she knew the score. "Surely your man has a gun."

"He does. But using it in a residential street...we'd rather not unless we absolutely have to."

She stroked the business card Greg had given to her earlier. She'd used up all the money her husband had accrued during their marriage and now survived on a private pension. It was enough, but not for the kinds of things she wanted. She planned to cash in on this little episode. She'd ask for small bits and bobs and started with, "I've seen some nice shoes on my computer."

A sigh. "How much do they cost?"

"Ninety-five pounds."

"Someone will bring it round later, you bloody chancer."

Ida laughed at the line going dead. This was like the old days, being in the thick of it, when she'd ridden pillion on The Blade's Vespa, the wind in her face, the pair of them off to some fight or other where she'd stand and watch her husband beat seven bells out of someone for Ron Cardigan.

She was useful again, and, fuelled by adrenaline, she made for the front door, eager to annoy Steve, one of her favourite pastimes.

Oh, for fuck's sake.

She was here again, that bloody nosy Mrs Greaves, coming out of her house and waggling her arm at Steve. What did she fucking want *now*?

"I saw your Albie," she said.

Well, he hadn't expected her to say that. Maybe speaking to her wouldn't be so bad after all. "When? Where?"

"Just now. He's not long left."

Why did he come here? "Are you sure it was him?"

"Of course I am. I came out and spoke to him."

Steve calculated the timings in his head. Yeah, Albie could have left the flat in the red car, got dropped off, all in the minutes that had passed since Steve had gone to The Glass Shard. Had he brought the big man with him?

"What did he say?" he asked.

Mrs Greaves shrugged. "Just that he wanted to see you. I told him you went out."

"Was he with anyone?" He adjusted his jacket fronts to ensure she wouldn't see the gun in his waistband.

She folded her arms. "No, he was on his own."

"Did he get out of a car? A red one?"

She squinted. "Not that I saw. He was walking down the street, that's why I saw him."

"Which direction did he go in?"

Mrs Greaves appeared alarmed, then her expression snapped into her usual one. "No need to go after him, he'll be back in a minute. He's just nipped to the shops. Going to buy you a bottle of whiskey, he said."

Steve hid a smile. Had Albie realised it was pointless running? Had he helped the big man escape then come here? Or was this old biddy giving him a load of crap?

Why would she? She doesn't know anything's going on.

She had to be telling the truth.

The whiskey. Albie knew it was Steve's favourite. Perhaps he'd come to his senses after the scare of being kidnapped and coming home was the natural thing to do.

He looked at Mrs Greaves for her to continue.

"He said he's been living on the other side of the East End all this time," she went on. "So near yet so far. I'm surprised you haven't bumped into each other. I mean, what are the chances that you didn't? He's got himself a job, although he didn't say what it was."

I bet he didn't, the filthy little bastard. "That's good to hear, at least he hasn't been going hungry. What else did he have to say for himself?" He wouldn't put it past the woman to be toying with him, Albie telling her about being kidnapped and whatever, her biding her time until she let him know she was aware of everything. What if she'd already phoned the police and she kept him talking until they got here?

Mrs Greaves pursed her lips. "Oh, you know, that he's settled where he is and just wanted to explain why he ran away. I suppose he's had an attack of conscience. That happens, doesn't it, when you get older. You look back and realise some of your actions weren't the best."

Was that a dig at me, or am I being paranoid?

"True." How many times had Steve done that lately, thinking about his choices? *Too many.* "Right, I may as well go in and wait for him, then."

"Oh, don't do that. Come to mine. I said I'd be one of those intermediary people or whatever they're called. You know, a mediator, in case you have a row."

Steve supposed that would work and...hold up, was she implying he had a temper and might start on Albie? Had she heard more than he'd thought over the years? Whatever, it would be better than staying in his house where the police could find him. If they turned up while he was in Mrs Greaves', he'd force her to help him escape. Send her out the front to keep them chatting while he legged it out the back. "I've just got to nip inside a sec, then I'll be round."

"I'll wait here for you."

Steve frowned at her smiling across the road. He turned to check if a neighbour was out, but no one appeared to be around. *Fucking loony.* He went inside, found his passport, and thought about some nice bits of jewellery in the office he could take with him and sell in Spain. The cash would tide him over; best not to access his bank accounts while he was away.

He stepped outside and had second thoughts about going into the old woman's place. It didn't feel right, his gut was warning him something was off, so he walked past her house, ignoring her calling him back, and headed towards the shops. He could intercept Albie on his way here, make out he was sorry for everything he'd done, get the

247

lad on his side again. He'd pretended well enough when he'd first met Karen and could do it again.

He stepped out onto the road, ready to cross it, gauging whether he could get over in time before a fast-moving van got too close. He chanced it, putting on a burst of speed, and the van did the same.

Realisation hit him at the same time he walloped onto the van's bonnet, his head smacking on the windscreen. He bounced off, flew through the air, and landed on the road, every bone and muscle screaming from the impact. Through gauzy vision, he stared at the side of the van.

BETTY'S CAKES.

He was well and truly fucked, and Mrs Greaves' distant, cackling laughter confirmed it.

Chapter Eighteen

*T*he next knock on the door came when Albie had been in the flat for a month. He stared through the peephole at Dad and Muttley, and the fact his father had brought reinforcements along gave Albie the collywobbles. It was just after one o'clock on a Sunday afternoon, and Albie had been opening the windows as the summer had been a hot one so far. They might have seen that from outside, so they'd know someone was either in here now or had nipped out and would be coming back. Thankfully, the telly wasn't on, Albie had been in the kitchen cooking when the knock had sounded, but it was obvious someone was living here.

Albie stared at the man who'd brought him up, although that term was stretching it. Shouted instructions and thumps weren't exactly 'bringing up' material, were they. Dad looked haggard, as if the murder had infected him and ravaged his features. Good. He deserved to feel guilty, to worry about the police coming round. Albie didn't think for one minute Dad had been worried about him, and that was why he seemed so beaten.

Another knock, and Muttley stepped out of sight. A softer knock, possibly on the flat next door, had Albie frantic with nerves. Whoever lived there might say they'd heard someone moving around. Fucking hell.

"Albie, are you in there?" Dad said. "Come on, son, stop being daft."

Was he just guessing? If he'd been watching the block, he wouldn't have seen Albie coming and going because he hadn't left the flat since he'd arrived, but he could have seen him at the window on his many checks to make sure Dad wasn't standing on the pavement. Dad or Muttley could have been sitting in a car up the road, far enough away that Albie wouldn't spot them.

"Look, we need you for a job, all right?" Dad said.

And there it was, the only reason they were here. To get him to go to bloody work for them. Even though Albie had told himself he didn't care if Dad wasn't bothered about his absence, it still stung. Would he always want his father to show he cared, even though he blatantly didn't? Why, when Albie had been treated so poorly, did he need some kind of validation that he mattered? Mattered more than being the person who climbed through windows and opened front doors?

Or was this a ruse? They didn't need him for a job at all and had come to cart him home so Dad could kill him.

The thought of that weakened Albie's knees, and he almost reached out to take the chain off, draw the bolts across out of habit, out of needing to obey. But he had Karen's clothes and makeup on, and opening the door like this would add fuel to an already raging inferno.

He didn't believe Dad and Muttley hadn't gone on any jobs for the month Albie had been here. Or maybe they hadn't because Dad had been lying low after the murder. Who cared anyway? Albie was never going back, would never let on he stood here now, wishing they'd just fuck off.

Muttley came back. "Someone's in there, but the woman next door doesn't know who."

251

Albie pressed his ear to the door by the hinges to hear them better.

"Karen hasn't got any family," Dad said, "and no one knows what happened to her, so as far as anyone's concerned, she's still alive."

"Listen, for all you know, she could have been keeping things from you. She might have rented it to someone when she lived with you, maybe she went with an estate agent to deal with it all. Sorry, but I can't see Albie being here. He's not as thick as you make out. Why would he come here when he knows this is the first place you'd look? And think about it, like I said on the way over, how did he get a key or know the address?"

"She must have told him where the flat is and given him a bloody key. She'd been acting weird for a few weeks before...before it all kicked off."

"We'll just have to recruit someone else for Albie's job. Face it, he's in the wind, he's not coming back. What happened probably scared him shitless, and he knows well enough to keep his mouth shut. It's been a month, and no one's come round to your place apart from that doctor fella. If Albie tells the police, he only gets himself in the shit, so chill out."

"I know all that, but he's mine."

"You haven't exactly been bothered by him being around except for work, so I'd have thought him being gone was a Godsend."

"No, you don't get it. He's mine. He belongs to me. Doesn't matter whether I hate him or not. I want to speak to him to tell him what'll happen if he blabs."

"He already knows, trust me."

"If he's not here, where the fuck has he gone?"

"Who knows? Homeless most likely. Maybe he's become a rent boy." Muttley's laughter sounded wheezy.

"Wouldn't surprise me. He's a woolly-woofer through and through. Disgusting."

Albie shouldn't be hurt, not after all these years of being called names, but he was nonetheless. He wasn't gay, he wasn't anything in the sex department, he was just himself. Herself. And, according to Dad, disgusting.

"Fuck this for a game of soldiers," Muttley said. "I'm not wasting any more time on him. He's gone, accept it, and we need to find another kid. Maybe Jacob's boy will be up for it. The lad's been nicking from shops for ages."

"But he won't do my washing and cook my dinner, will he."

Albie shook his head. Dad was such an arsehole.

"Come on," Muttley said.

"I'll find him in the end, you mark my words." Dad again. "He won't be able to stay hidden forever."

Albie's guts churned, and he slowly peeled himself off the door and looked through the peephole. Dad and Muttley walked away, towards the stairs, then Dad turned to glance over his shoulder.

"I swear I could smell him through that door."

Albie swallowed, his chest tight. Would they stay away now? Or would Dad come back for another go? When Albie finally left here, he'd have to do it in the dark. Dad might be watching during the day.

Albie had a lot to think about.

The first red letter came a month later. The electricity company wanted their money, Karen's direct debit had bounced, and if it wasn't paid by the end of October, they were cutting her off. That gave Albie some leeway, he could stay here until the lights went out, but he'd be cold, the winter settling in by then, and he wouldn't be able to cook. The appliances were all electric, as was the heating. He took a risk and went out to buy a camping stove and gas, ready for when his world turned dark. He picked up some food, mainly tins and more pasta, hating having to use some of his escape fund, but it was either that or starve. The relief upon returning to the flat and locking himself in was immense. The whole time he'd been out, he'd expected Dad to jump out from around a corner and drag him back home.

Albie had received stares, some curious, some disgusted. He'd gone out in Karen's clothes and makeup, although he'd put his trainers on because Karen's shoes were a tad too small, only okay for wearing in the flat. It had been a novel experience, being a girl out in the open, frightening on one hand, comforting on the other. His hair had grown, and he reckoned he 'passed' as a female. One day he'd get permanent hair extensions, blonde, and clothes that fitted him properly.

For now, he'd make do.

The electricity had been cut off on the date stated on the red letter, and the water bill had arrived, due to be settled in December. If it wasn't for this place being on Dad's radar, Albie would have found work so he could pay both bills out of his savings, but he was too afraid to leave the flat often, only going out to replace the gas bottle, pick up more tins, buy loo roll and some cheap candles and matches. The TV licence was due to be renewed in January, but with no electric, he hadn't even had the telly for entertainment. He'd nipped into a charity shop and bought a load of books for seventy pence each, thick ones that would last him ages, discovering the joys of Tolkien.

November had come around, cold and bleak, and he spent his days reading, wrapped in layers of Karen's clothes with her fluffy throw blanket around him when he sat on the sofa. He'd had so much time to think, memories encroaching in the dead of night, pulling him from sleep and keeping him awake.

His nightmares consisted of Karen being murdered over and over again, and they went on to show him what his subconscious thought had happened to her afterwards. Dad driving to the countryside, not to the sea like he'd told Mrs Greaves, and finding some thick forest in the middle of nowhere. He parked up, keeping his headlights on so he could see what he was doing when he dug a deep hole, so deep that with Dad inside it as he tossed mud out, only his head had poked up come the end. Karen's body wasn't intact in his dreams but cut up, arms, legs, head, and torso separate pieces, all coated in blood, her eyes missing, her tongue sticking out, thick and blue and so terrible. Dad slung *the parts of her into the hole one by one, telling her what a stupid cow she was and if she'd just behaved, she wouldn't be lying in the mud with the worms.*

Albie stood as a spectator, unable to intervene, his feet stuck to the forest floor. Birds had come awake in the darkness, roused by Dad's words, and some flew into the hole and pecked at Karen, their beaks scarlet, her flesh dangling from them. Dad flapped his hands to shoo them away, and they obeyed, like Albie and Karen had once done, floating out of the grave to hover, vultures, waiting for Dad to leave.

He filled the hole, grumbling about it hurting his back, and patted the mud down once he'd completed the task. He dragged mulch and twigs and leaves over, disguising Karen's resting place, then paused, cocking his head.

"I can smell you, kid."

Albie tried to run, but vines came up from the ground and held him fast.

"I know you're here somewhere. Come out so you can do a job."

Dad turned. Spotted him. Came towards him.

Albie always woke at that point, sweating, too hot, his heart beating so fast he couldn't take a breath. He'd convinced himself this was a portent, that Dad would catch up with him eventually.

A knock at the door had him bounding off the sofa, flinging the blanket off him and tiptoeing to the peephole. Dad stood there, no Muttley in sight, hands on hips, the scowl of old wrinkling his forehead and bunching his eyebrows.

"Albie, open up."

Had he been watching? Had he seen him going out at the arse crack of dawn this morning to buy gas? The place on the industrial estate that sold it opened at seven-thirty, and it had still been dark. He'd thought he'd been safe.

"Look, kid, I know you're in there, so stop fucking me about."

Albie shook all over.

"You don't have to do jobs anymore, we've got a new lad, but I just want to talk about…what happened that night. I need to know you're going to keep your gob shut."

Albie did just that, folding his lips over his teeth.

"I can't be doing with going in the nick, and I don't think you'd be any good in there, what with all that gayness. They'll be up your backside quicker than you can blink. They can smell a bender a mile away."

Albie blinked back tears.

"Just knock on the door to tell me you're going to keep this quiet."

Albie stuffed his fists beneath his armpits.

"Ah, fuck you," Dad shouted. "Just fuck you, you gay little bastard."

He stomped off to the stairs and disappeared down them. Albie leant on the wall and let the tears fall. His time was limited here now. Dad knew *he was here somehow, and it was too dangerous to stay. Albie had planned to remain here until the spring, he had enough money for his tins of beans and packets of pasta, because being homeless on the streets of London in the cold wasn't something he wanted to go through.*

He rushed to the living room and peeked out of a gap in the curtains. Dad still had the same car, and he got in it, the headlights splashing onto the blue Mini in front. He looked up at the window, shook his head, and drove away.

April. That was all Albie needed to get to. Then he could disappear.

Chapter Nineteen

Aster sat in a 'quiet room' at the clinic with Alien who'd bought her a sandwich and a cup of hot chocolate. It was all very well, sitting here, but she needed to know what was happening about Dad.

She had to be content that she was safe. Moon had just left, having told her she'd be taken to one of his safe houses, located out of London. He'd taken Sarah with him, who'd only had a flesh wound that had been cleaned and sewn up already. Aster hadn't asked where he was taking her so-called friend—she hadn't cared enough to bother. What Sarah had done was stupid, could have resulted in Brickhouse being dead if that bullet had hit the main artery in his leg, something one of the nurses had come out to tell them after his initial assessment.

He was 'lucky', according to her, and he'd be in surgery for a while yet. The bullet had lodged in a muscle, bypassing the bones. After he'd been shot, shock had him passing out, otherwise, he'd said, he would have got straight up and driven Aster and Sarah away.

"You okay?" Alien asked.

"Just thinking how it could have gone the other way. My dad mentioned the word 'conversion' when we were in the flat. I keep asking myself what it means."

"Could be anything," Alien said. "I wouldn't even waste time thinking about it."

A knock on the door had her looking through the small square of glass in the top. George's face filled the space, minus his fake beard and eyebrows. He entered scratching his chin and complaining about the glue giving him the itches. Greg followed, his beard still in place. They looked odd in tracksuits.

"I ran the fucker over," George said. "Your dad."

Relief had Aster sagging. "Where is he?"

"At the warehouse. I knocked him down, but the silly prick got back up and ran down the road. I whacked into him again and rolled over his legs."

Aster couldn't believe how blasé George was, how what he'd done seemed so *normal* to him.

"Bit of a fucking crunch he made." He sat on a chair. "That's three people we need to deal with at the warehouse now, plus that Sarah bint, although Moon said he can help out with her."

Aster should have known Sarah wouldn't get away lightly. "What are you going to do with her?"

"She sold you out for money, so what do you think?"

Greg sat beside his brother. "We'll know more about her when we speak to Norton again."

Aster sat up straighter. "You got *him* as well?"

George nodded. "Collared him in a pub."

Alien chuckled. "Martin's babysitting, I take it."

Greg leant back. "Yeah. Will's gone to sit with him, seeing as he's not needed at Steve's anymore."

"So I don't need to go to Moon's safe house?" Aster asked.

George nodded. "I'd prefer for you to be out of the way until this is all over. We've got a proposition for you. When this is all over, move into one of our vacant flats. We'll set up a panic alarm in case you need it. You mentioned a bloke called Muttley. What if he comes after you?"

"He won't."

"How can you be so sure?"

"I just can." She hadn't told them or Debbie about him. What had happened. "Where's the flat?"

"Down the road from The Angel." George studied her intently. "Do you like your job, or is it just a means to an end?"

"I can't stand it, but it brings the money in so…"

"We'll find you something else to do."

"Like what?"

"Dunno, let me think about it. The question I want answered now is: Do you want to come to the warehouse in the morning and speak to your dad before I kill him?"

"No, I never want to see him again." Aster had dreamt of murdering her father so many times, but now it had come down to the wire, she didn't want to witness it. She couldn't be doing with even more horror living inside her head.

"Fine. Well, all that's left is for you to move into your new flat then once everyone's in the Thames. Our men will pack your gear, so until the police have finished sniffing round your area—they're looking for whoever shot Sarah, someone reported it—you can go to Moon's safe place with Alien."

It seemed weird, for it all to be over just like that, no fanfare, a bit of a damp squib, but did Aster *want* any extra hassle? No, she'd suffered enough, and a bit of quiet time would do her the world of good.

She stood at the same time as Alien who put an arm around her shoulder. "Come on, girl, let's be off."

Girl. He'd called her girl.

Aster smiled all the way to his car.

"Why tomorrow?" Greg asked. "Why aren't we killing the lot of them tonight?"

George had already anticipated his twin asking that and had come up with a plausible answer. "We've been on the go all fucking day, and I've got a date with Janet tonight, plus, the hours will give them all time to think about things. The longer they're lost in thought, the more likely they'll open up to us. I don't fancy trying to get blood out of a stone."

Greg eyed him as if he knew he was lying out of his arse. "Makes a change. It's usually what you hope for, them being awkward so you can hurt them."

"Can't be bothered, bruv."

Greg shrugged. "Fair enough. I'll stick around for when Brickhouse wakes up, shall I, seeing as you meeting Janet is more important."

A squeeze of guilt wrenched at George. Normally, they'd do that together, sitting here until Brickhouse was in the recovery room. Was Ruffian just as much of a bully as Mad, pushing George to go out there and kill someone?

"If you wouldn't mind," he said.

"Of course I fucking mind, else I wouldn't have said anything, would I?"

"Christ, keep your wig on."

Greg snatched it off and rolled it into a ball. "No."

George laughed. "Pack it in being such a dick."

Greg sat back, arms folded. "Go on, piss off to your missus."

George walked out, saying over his shoulder, "You'll need to get a lift back home. I'm taking the van."

"Tosser."

George smiled and left the clinic, too busy listening to Ruffian, who put forward a pretty decent suggestion. George nodded in answer and drove away, glad the darkness wouldn't be long in coming.

Chapter Twenty

*A*t half past five on a Friday evening, the April air sharp, the grip on the back of Albie's neck meant only one thing. He froze in the can aisle of Tesco, his hand on a tin of beans, his other occupied by holding a basket.

"I don't want any trouble, so put those down and come with me."

Dad's voice was so close from behind, his breath hot, seeping through Albie's longer, thicker hair. His first instinct was to obey, but he fought back that urge and put the beans in his basket as though his father's hold wasn't anything to worry about. He shrugged to indicate Dad ought to let him go, and surprisingly, he did.

"Don't even think of screaming like a girl or making a run for it."

Despite fear flouncing through him, Albie walked along to the spaghetti hoops and put one in his basket. He went farther, to the mushy peas, then decided he didn't want them. They reminded him of chippy nights with Dad and the first big payday when Muttley had also bought gravy and those slices of cake.

"Don't you fucking ignore me," Dad said, following along. "I've got shitloads on you, so you'd be better off doing as you're told and coming outside with me."

"I've got shitloads on you, too, so piss off."

Albie couldn't believe he'd said that, he'd only meant to think it, but so what if he did make his feelings clear? What could Dad do in a busy supermarket? Then the realisation of what he could do outside slammed into Albie, and he regretted his words. Dad would wait out there, hours if need be, until Albie emerged.

"Look," Albie said, not looking at his father, instead staring at some canned mushrooms, "if you're worried about me saying anything, don't. I could have done it months ago and didn't. We're both in the shit if the police are involved. I'd be stupid to open my mouth. That's all you want to know, isn't it? Whether the murder you committed will get out?"

"Shut your fat fucking mouth, you bell-end. People will hear you."

"You're scared, aren't you."

"The fuck I am."

Albie walked off, turned the corner, and entered the pasta aisle. He acted as if his stomach wasn't doing somersaults, that his chest wasn't tight from fear, and that he didn't need to go to the toilet because his bowels had caught up to the fact Dad had found him and needed to vacate. He picked up pasta shells and added them to his basket.

"You're in her flat, aren't you," Dad said.

He was so near, the heat from his body brought out goosebumps on Albie's arms. Albie moved along to the linguine.

"Did you have a cold winter with no electric? I saw the lights weren't on. Reckon you've got candles, maybe a torch."

So he had been watching. That was no surprise. Why had Dad waited this long to approach him? There had been numerous times Albie had left the flat. Maybe Dad was sticking to his routine as much as possible because Mrs Greaves had become nosier. Who knew.

"Go away," Albie said. "You don't need to know where I am, just that I'm keeping it all quiet and you're safe, so do yourself a favour and sod off."

The hand on his arm, spinning him around, was expected. Albie stared into his father's eyes, resisting the need to spit in his face.

"If you don't let me go, I'll scream and tell everyone you killed my mum and Karen. I'll say you forced me to break into those houses and put her in that suitcase. Yeah, I'll probably go down for it, but it'll be worth it to know you're banged up and can't come near me anymore."

"You wouldn't dare."

"Do you want to try it?" It was so weird, standing up for himself, that it felt like someone else inhabited him. This out-of-body experience was alien, and old fears crept back in, ones he'd thought he'd banished while living in the flat. Still, he maintained the illusion

272

of being strong and unafraid. "Because I'm quite happy to blurt it all out to that old boy over there."

Dad glanced behind him at a fella reaching up for some rice. He turned back to face Albie. "You'd better not be fucking me about. Gob shut, got it?"

Albie shrugged. "Take your hand off me, then I'll keep it quiet."

Dad didn't like being told what to do, and it was clear he struggled with obeying the son he despised. But he removed his hand, stuffed it in his pocket, and glared. It still had the power to send Albie to his knees, that glare, but he stood firm.

"Leave me alone. I never want to see you again."

"That's not your decision," Dad said, miming a gun pointing at Albie, then stalked off.

Albie wandered towards the old man, his instinct to be close to someone who represented safety, then, after a minute or so staring at labels with Long Grain and Pilau on them, he went to the till, watching for Dad, preparing himself for another confrontation outside.

He paid and left the shop, going to sit on one of the benches nearby, where he scoured the car park for Dad's car and didn't get up until he was satisfied it had gone. On the way back to Karen's, he popped into the chippy, splurging by buying a pie to go with his chips. He ate them leaning against the shop, thinking a pie would always remind his of this day, the day he'd finally stood up for himself against a man who'd frightened him all his life.

And it felt good.

Albie walked across the grass towards the high-rise, anxious that Dad might be around, lurking, watching. Would that feeling ever go away, even when he moved on from here? He didn't believe Dad would just let this go, let him go, no matter that he'd seemed okay with Albie saying he wouldn't blurt anything.

He pushed the main door, lifting one foot to step inside, but a hand on the back of his neck stopped him. His first thought was that it was Dad again, but the hand felt different. Bigger. The fingertips reached farther round his neck than his father's, and whoever it was had gloves on. Albie kicked back, his shoe connecting with what he thought was a shin, and the person who held him let go. Albie spun round and came face to face with Muttley.

"I've seen my dad not long ago, so there's no need for you to stick your oar in, too," Albie said, pleased with the splash of shock on Muttley's face; he wouldn't have expected Albie to talk to him like that. "We came to an agreement. I keep my mouth shut, and he leaves me alone. Same goes for you."

Muttley jerked his head to the side. "Let's talk down here." He wandered to the gap between the high-rises, the dark swallowing him up.

"Are you joking me?" Albie put one foot inside again.

"Look..." The word floated out of the blackness. "He's going off the rails, and I need your help to get him committed."

Albie frowned. "Committed to what, another mad scheme of yours?"

"No, the fucking nuthouse, you pleb. He's off his tree, and a family member has to ask for him to be carted away."

Dad had lost his marbles? Albie didn't believe that. "Pull the other one."

"I mean it. He's not right up top, his brain's gone."

"So why can't we discuss it here, where there's light? I mean, he could be hiding down there, and you two plan on kidnapping me or something."

Muttley stepped out of the murk, hands in his jacket pockets. "Okay, I'll come clean. He is mental, he does need putting away, but the truth is, I need you for jobs. What about me ditching him, then me and you work together?"

Albie wasn't having any of that. Stealing was his past, not his future. "Err, how about no."

Muttley darted forward and grabbed Albie's hair, fingers tightening on either side of his head. "Listen to me, you little shit. I've had a bellyful since you fucked off, your old man griping in my ear, not to mention the burials he roped me into when I didn't want anything to do with it."

Mum and Karen? *"Get off me or I'll scream."*

"Scream and I'll slit your throat." Muttley let go with one hand and slid it into his pocket, producing a knife. He flicked the blade out of the handle and held it at Albie's neck. "Does this make everything clearer now? Does it prove I mean business?"

Albie dropped his bag of shopping, preparing himself to fight. "Why can't you just leave me alone?"

"Because you know too much."

"I've told Dad I won't be saying anything. I want out. I never wanted to do it in the first place."

"No, you can't get out. You're too useful. You know the rules. We can't be doing with teaching anyone else. We don't trust anyone but you."

"You did it on your own for long enough after he killed my mum, so do it again."

Muttley increased the pressure on the blade. "You don't get to choose. You don't have a choice. You're coming with me now, and I swear to God, if we have to chain you up in that office all the time until we go out on jobs, then that's what we'll do."

The fear of that, the brass neck of the suggestion, bought on rage so blinding, Albie didn't know what to do with himself. His face heated, and his pulse throbbed at his temples. He raised his hands slowly, bringing them up together between them, then opened them quickly. The movement caught Muttley off-guard, his knife arm swinging away to the side. Albie took his chance and planted his hands on Muttley's chest, shoving him backwards. Muttley staggered, letting out a harsh "You fucking wanker!", then he vanished into the gloom. A loud, sickening thud floated towards Albie, and he stood there shaking, his breathing heavy, glancing about to see if anyone was around who had seen what had happened.

No one, not even a person at a window. All the curtains of the houses opposite were closed. He let out a small sigh of relief and braced himself for Muttley to appear and charge at him, but he didn't.

Did that thud mean…? Oh fuck, had something happened to him?

Albie switched his phone on to get light from the screen. He crept towards where Muttley had disappeared, and the meagre beam showcased

Muttley's shoe. The phone screen darkened, and Albie lit it up again, panning it upwards until he reached Muttley's face. Shit, there was blood, a lot of it. Muttley's head was at a weird angle and, just as Albie moved closer to see what had happened, his bloody phone doused again. Once more, he fired it up. Muttley had landed on the rockery border of the path, and it looked like the point of a large stone had sunk into his skull.

What should he do? Phone the police? Go inside and pretend it hadn't happened? Albie glanced around again, searching for anyone who could have witnessed what had gone on. Still no one. He stuffed his phone away and backed into the light coming from the foyer, the sight of the knife catching his attention. He picked it up—it might have his DNA on it from where it had been pressed to his neck—and flicked the blade into the handle. Mind made up, he snatched up his bag of shopping and walked into the building, rushing to Karen's flat. Inside, he locked the door and leant against it.

He'd probably killed Muttley.

How the hell would he get out of this?

The rapid knock came at seven fifty-nine a.m., the numbers on the bedside clock a glowing green. It took a moment for Albie to remember where he was and what had occurred, but the reality of it thumped into his head in nasty boots and propelled him out of bed. Another knock, and he reckoned it was the police, especially if Muttley was dead.

Before sleep had finally taken him, he'd prayed that Muttley had just been knocked out and had come to, getting up and driving away. Could that still be the case and Dad was here instead, ready to give Albie a bollocking?

He stumbled into the hallway and stared through the peephole.

A policeman in uniform stood there.

Albie swallowed and drew the chain across. He could do this. Act like he had with Karen's colleague that time. It would be okay.

He opened the door.

"Hello, sorry to be here so early." The copper grinned. "You look like I just woke you up. We're doing house-to-house enquiries regarding a fatal accident. Can I ask you a couple of questions? It won't take long, just routine."

Accident? Routine? Albie relaxed. "Err, okay."

"Did you go out anywhere at all yesterday evening?"

"I went to Tesco, yeah. Got a bit of shopping in."

"Ah, that might explain a tin of beans found out the front."

"Beans?" Jesus Christ, fucking hell, shit. "Oh, I dropped my bag, so maybe it rolled out."

"Why did you drop it?" The copper wrote something down in his notebook.

"I was getting my keys out of my pocket at the same time as pushing the main door open."

"Sausage fingers."

Albie laughed and hoped he didn't sound nervous. "Yeah."

"What time did you get back?"

Albie reckoned adding fifteen minutes to his original time would work. It was plausible that he'd have walked past a dead Muttley, seeing as he was in the dark. "About half six, something like that."

"Did you notice anyone outside on the path?"

He pulled a face. "No. There wasn't anyone around when I got back."

"Okay. Did you hear anything after you came to your flat? A scuffle or an argument?"

"No."

"What about before you left. What time was that?"

"I went about quarter to five. I didn't hear anything or see anyone other than the woman in the house opposite, the one with the full glass door. She mentioned the weather to me."

"That's fine. Thanks for your time."

Albie closed the door and sank to the floor. Fucking hell. Fatal must mean Muttley was dead. Albie couldn't stay here anymore. He'd have to leave, make his way elsewhere. It was going to be a long road, but he had no choice. This flat was too dangerous, and once Dad found out Muttley had died, he'd be round here like a shot.

In the living room, he stared down at a white tent where Muttley had fallen. Someone must have discovered him this morning on their way to work. It would still have been dark, but not as much as last night. He shuddered at the thought of the body, at the rock sticking into Muttley's head.

Albie would leave once the police had gone. Maybe tomorrow, once those forensic people who currently walked all over the grass had finished their jobs. For now, he went into the kitchen to make some tea and think about his future.

One that looked incredibly bleak.

Chapter Twenty-One

Two date nights in a row couldn't have come at a better time. Normally, there were a couple of days in between, but Janet had a conference in Wales tomorrow, extending until the weekend, so they'd switched to tonight. It suited George, because since he'd become Ruffian, he had a new devil on his shoulder, urging him to rid the East End of scum. Small-time scum for now, he reckoned; it would prevent those who could grow into even bigger scum, given the chance, from even getting to that stage.

"How was your day?" he asked his plate of scampi, unable to look Janet in the eye at the moment.

She'd been staring at him funny ever since they'd taken their seats in the corner of Budgie Smugglers, a gastro effort Up West. His chips, in a poncy metal bucket, reminded him of why he hated places like this. Give him chips in a paper packet any day, and as for the little tubs of tomato sauce…

Janet sighed. "Are you asking your food or me?"

He raised his head. "You."

"What's the matter? You're distracted, like you used to be when you first came to see me."

"Nothing's the matter." He speared a piece of scampi with his fork.

"Bullshit," she muttered. "My day was okay, as it happens. Well, if you don't count the client I had first thing, but it's a discussion that's off the table."

"Why, because you can't talk about their business?"

"Yes. I don't even get why you said that. You *know* how it goes."

"So what are you therapists meant to talk about when you discuss work like other people do? Is our relationship always going to have secrets?" He wanted her to say yes, so what he was doing behind everyone's backs was deemed okay. If she could hide shit, so could he.

She twirled spaghetti around her fork. "I wouldn't call them secrets, more like things I can't reveal."

That'll do for me. "I get it. I have the same thing going on."

"Hmm, but yours are illegal, mine aren't."

"Yet here you are."

She sometimes poked at him for being a criminal, but she never turned down a chance to meet up with him. She was a walking contradiction, and he thought *she* needed therapy, considering.

They ate for a while in a comfortable silence, George contemplating his antics once he left here, anticipating prowling and seeing someone doing wrong, him sorting it. He'd come here in the fake taxi, a new number plate and cab licence on the back, his disguise inside a rucksack in the passenger footwell. The car park to this place was at the rear, so he'd have plenty of privacy to sort himself out.

"What are you thinking?" She pushed her plate aside. She'd had carbonara and a side of garlic bread.

"About last night," he lied. "I mean, you stormed out, so aren't we meant to not be talking after a ding-dong? Isn't that how it works? See how long the other one can ignore you?"

"The storm-out was me making a point, and you know it," she said, "otherwise, neither of us would be here now, would we."

"What was the point of the point then?"

"To show you that I don't have to listen to your stubborn arse if I don't want to. I can remove myself from the situation at any time, plus, it was our first row, as you put it, so that wouldn't be complete without me walking away. If you remember, I said me huffing off was so it matched your idea of what a relationship is. What I was showing was I'm prepared to do things like that so you're more comfortable."

"And storming out fits the bill, does it?"

"Yes, if that's what you'd expect."

He shook his head. "Seems a bit fucked-up to me. I didn't have you down as someone who'd pander to a bloke, to do things you wouldn't normally do to please him."

She laughed, although it was clear she wasn't amused. "I do so many things to please you, and don't even bother letting your mind go into the gutter, that's not what we're discussing. I *know* who you are and what you do, yet I haven't phoned the police. At first it was client confidentiality, and now… Well, I'm caught up in you, aren't I, I've gone down the classic route of turning a blind eye for love, and it could well get me into trouble. I imagine one day I'll lose my licence if it ever gets out that I know stuff and didn't say."

"Then we'll employ you to be a therapist to our employees and residents only. You get to keep your licence because the higher-ups won't be any the wiser as to what you're doing in 'pleasing' me, keeping my secrets safe. All people who come to see you will be given a warning about not telling anyone they've even *been* to see you. Easy."

"But I love running my own practice."

"You can still run it, just not for your usual clients, and you can get rid of your secretary. Aster can take her place."

"Aster."

"The woman we're helping at the moment."

"Will you match my earnings?"

"We'll double it."

She picked up the dessert menu and browsed. "The chocolate cake looks nice."

"Now who's deflecting."

She lowered the menu. "Because I'm trying to come to grips with the fact that if I take you up on your offer, I'll have stepped out of a sort of ethical life and into an unethical one."

"I don't see it that way. You'd still be helping people."

"I'll have to think about it." She stared at the list of puddings again. "I suppose you'll be having the apple crumble."

"Yep, so long as there's custard. Ice cream hurts my teeth."

"It would mean turning away NHS referrals," she said.

"There are other therapists who can take up the slack."

"I have people who trust me, and it might set them back if I don't see them."

"Look, this is all your choice. You moan you might lose your licence if you're associated with me and my shit, I give you a solution—where you're a damn sight richer, I might add—and you put up roadblocks." He shrugged. "Your call. If you feel you need to walk away from me, do it now before—"

"Before what?"

We're not going there. "It doesn't matter."

"Before you get too close to me?"

Bog off, Janet. "Have they got any profiteroles on there? I fancy two puds."

"They do."

He relaxed now they were off dodgy ground. "Have you made your mind up about the chocolate cake?"

"What, about having my cake and eating it?"

"Yeah."

"Not yet."

George leant back. He enjoyed these chats, where they changed the subject yet at the same time stayed on the same one, just using different words to convey things. Janet was one hundred percent his type of woman, and it'd be a shame if she severed contact just because he'd killed a few people. *I mean, that's not a big deal, me being a murderer, is it?* Still, like he'd implied, she'd better do it sooner rather than later. This bird had fair got under his skin, and he didn't much like the prospect of having to get her out if she walked away. It'd likely hurt.

"I'll tell you about the cake tomorrow," she said, "when I've slept on it."

"If you sleep on cake, it makes a mess of the sheets."

"You're telling me not to overthink it."

"Yep. Don't make a mess of something that's so simple."

He caught the eye of a server walking by and asked if they could order dessert. While they waited, Janet likely pondering his offer, George congratulated himself on a good idea. If their employees and any residents who needed help got it for free on their dime, then ended up lighter of spirit for it, it had to be the way to go, didn't it? Greg would agree, he usually did on this sort of thing. Martin, especially, could benefit from some one-on-one therapy.

The puddings arrived, and George tucked in.

Janet chewed on some chocolate cake. Swallowed. "This is lovely."

"Cake usually is. The one I'm offering has a cherry on the top."

"I know."

She smiled.

He smiled.

He'd won her over.

Chapter Twenty-Two

Janet had made it clear she wasn't up for him going back to her place for a couple of hours to use the sheets in a different way. She needed a good night's sleep, what with travelling tomorrow. George didn't mind, he wanted to get going as Ruffian. He waited for her to drive away, then pulled the rucksack from the footwell and took out a beard-and-eyebrow set. He'd gone for ginger again, the beard extra bushy, and the wig matched, all curls and frizz. He glanced at himself in the rearview, reckoned he looked like a demented leprechaun, and laughed, putting a puffa jacket on and removing his tie, the navy one he always opted for when going out with Janet. Zip drawn up, gloves on, he was ready to go.

The journey back to the East End took a while, even though he'd driven on the outskirts to avoid snags in traffic. Back on his own patch, he felt more comfortable, the familiar landmarks a balm to his soul. He cruised the streets of the Fielding housing estate, keeping an eye out for naughty no-marks who thought they were the bee's knees. Annoyed because no one appeared to be breaking any Cardigan laws, he went elsewhere, scouring an area with run-down houses, then drove behind them to the industrial estate.

A car had parked up outside a place that sold gear for arts and crafts, the windows steamed up. He switched his headlights off and cut the engine, letting the taxi coast up behind what he suspected was a Ford, going by the shape. He applied the handbrake, snatched up a tyre iron from the back seat, and got out, intending to scare the occupants for a laugh, but a muffled scream from inside had him on high alert.

He tried the Ford's door handle, but it wouldn't budge. Another scream, then someone snarling, "I said I'll pay you *after*, so just give me what I want."

George smacked the driver's-side window several times, the tyre iron eventually breaking the glass. No one sat in the front, so he glanced in the back.

"Help me!" a woman shouted. "Help!"

Incensed, Mad threatening to overtake his new persona, Ruffian reached inside and switched off the central locking. He wrenched the back door open and whacked the bloke on the back with the iron, the fella's pasty backside still going up and down despite that and the window being smashed. What had happened, he'd gone into such a frenzy to get what he wanted that he was unaware of what was going on?

Ruffian hit him again, and the man let out a roar. Putting the iron on top of the car, Ruffian lunged inside and grabbed the back of the twat's jacket. He hauled him out and threw him to the ground, kicking anywhere he could get the boot in. Guts, legs, head. He kept kicking, blood spurting, flesh splitting, teeth coming loose, his victim groaning and *oofing*, hands up to shield his face. The woman getting out of the car pulled Ruffian from his fun, and she stood there staring at him, then at the bloke.

"What happened?" Ruffian said.

"He wouldn't fucking pay me up front so decided to take what he wanted." She wiped her mascara-stained cheeks.

George peered past Ruffian's anger, recognising the woman as one of Debbie's night-time girls. "What are you doing this far away from the corner, Oralia?"

She backed away a little. "Who are you? How do you know my street name?"

He didn't like the way she looked at him, as if he scared her. He was all for being scary when dealing with people who'd done wrong, but not innocents, not a girl like this. Sod it, he'd have to come clean. "It's George."

She gawped at him, maybe wondering why he was as ginger as a biscuit. "W-where's Greg?" A glance to the taxi, then back to him. "You're on your own." She frowned.

"I was on my way back from somewhere. Is this prick one of your regulars?"

"No. He's a new one. I didn't…fuck, I didn't put him through the app you said we had to use."

"Now do you see why we insist on it?"

"Yeah."

He studied the punter. "He won't be anyone's regular for much longer."

"Shit. Shit. What are you…?"

"Get in the taxi. Wait until I've finished him off. The story goes to Debbie or the other girls, you weren't here. I wasn't here."

"Okay…"

"Have you got a police record, had to give them a DNA sample? Fingerprints?"

"No."

"Then you're safe. They won't know you were in that car."

It dawned on her what he was saying. This ponce would be found dead, and forensics would go through the Ford like a dose of salts.

"Oh God…" She walked in reverse, maintaining eye contact.

"On second thoughts," he said, "I'll torch the car. Oh, and shut your eyes if you don't want to see what I'm going to do to him."

Ruffian waited for her to get in the back of the taxi. She must have stretched out on the seat, because the dark shape of her head and shoulders wasn't visible. Ruffian eyed the units for CCTV. A couple had cameras, but it was too late now. They'd have captured him giving the prone man a kicking. He stepped forward and rested his shoe on the fella's neck, pressing hard, putting all of his weight on it. The soft crack of something breaking, almost unheard, a whisper in the night, had him smiling.

He set the stopwatch on his wrist for four minutes and stood that way, whistling, until the soft bleep alerted him that time was up. He didn't bother to check for a pulse. Instead, he grabbed the iron off the top of the car and battered the bloke's head with it, just to make sure he was dead.

This was one time he couldn't hide himself behind Ruffian's shroud. He'd have to warn Janine, tell Greg what he'd done.

Fuck it.

How would he explain being on the industrial estate, though?

He went back to the taxi, opening the boot and putting the iron in a carrier bag. He took out their can of petrol and doused the Ford's seats, then returned the can to the taxi boot. In their little tub of tricks, he found long matches and, at the car, he set the matchbox on fire and threw it onto the driver's seat. Back door closed, knowing the oxygen in the air that sailed through the broken window would feed the flames, he got in the taxi.

"Stay down until I get you home. Where do you live?"

She told him, then asked, "Is he dead?"

"Yeah." He drove away through smoke that billowed out of the window. "Our copper will sort it. I won't mention your name, but for God's sake, work savvy in future. Don't go with anyone who seems dodgy. *And use the app!*"

"But he didn't come off as weird. He was nice until it came to paying me."

"Bastard. And especially don't let punters take you to places like this. It's out of the way. He could have killed you. What has Debbie told you all about staying local? Only going a short distance from the corner? Did you tell any of the others where you'd be?"

"Yes. He said we'd park in the next street, but he kept going."

"And you didn't think to ring Debbie so she could get hold of us?"

"I didn't feel in danger. Like I told you, he was nice."

"Everyone can play nice when they want to." Ruffian seeped away, George taking his place. "Look, let this be a lesson, all right?"

She sat up and stared at him in the rearview. "I only do this to help pay for the fucking electric. I can't have my kiddies going cold."

George's heart went out to her. The rise in costs affected so many. "And that's the *only* reason you do it?"

"Do you think I *want* to? That I *enjoy* this bullshit?"

He sighed. Poor cow. "We'll pay your electric bills."

"What?"

"You heard me. Are you on a prepayment meter?"

"Yes."

"Then someone will drop round cash every week. I've got some on me to tide you over for now. In return, you'll give up the corner and become what we call our ears. You hear anything off, you tell us. I'll give you our number when we get to yours."

"Fucking hell, I don't know what to say."

"You don't say anything. Like I said, this never happened, got it?" He paused, realising that wouldn't work. He'd still have to explain why he'd been on the industrial estate. "Regarding Greg, you phoned me for help."

"But I don't have your number."

"We'll pretend you did."

She nodded, and he drove on, thinking of having to phone Janine and shitting all over her evening. It couldn't be helped.

He smiled to himself. Who said his alter egos weren't a good thing? If he hadn't become Ruffian, he wouldn't have driven down that road. Sometimes, fate showed you the way, and he was fucking glad it had. He'd killed a wanker and gained some ears.

Bargain.

"You've got blood on you, bruv." Greg stared at him from his chair in the living room. "And what's with going ginger?"

"There was a bit of trouble." George took the wig off and threw it on the roaring fire. He peeled

301

the beard and eyebrows away, lobbing them in, too.

"What kind of trouble?"

"Women trouble."

Greg shot forward. "Fuck me, you didn't kill *Janet*, did you?"

"Did I fuck." George stripped his clothes off and, reluctantly, added them to the flames. He even put his shoes on there, then positioned the guard in front. "That's another pair of expensive hoof covers wasted."

"Fuck the shoes. What's been going on?"

In just his boxers, George explained what had happened. "So we're paying her leccy bill from now on, and she'll be our ears, earning money that way."

"Poor bitch. She's a nice girl, too, Oralia."

"That's not her real name."

Greg rolled his eyes. "Obviously."

"She's called Zoe Callaghan, and she's got two kids. Boys. She's split from her fella."

"A wanker, is he?"

"Yeah. I've still got to let Janine know what's been going on, but I need a shower first."

George went upstairs, his mind percolating how else they could help Zoe. Some shopping maybe, delivered by Tesco. A bunch of flowers to cheer her up. Her reason for being out on the corner had really got to him, how she'd felt forced to open her legs to keep her children warm. She'd told him she had a day job in a clothes shop, and someone watched the kids in the evening while she'd plied the age-old trade. How many others on that corner, shit, the whole world over, had to sell themselves in order to survive? It sickened him. Still, at least he'd helped one of them get out.

He hoped she slept well tonight.

Janine stared down at the battered body of a male. Would she ever get used to sights like this? Ever understand how people could be so cruel to others? What she'd never get to grips with was people like George who *enjoyed* doing it. She thought he had a screw loose, personally, that he needed help, but she doubted he'd agree with her. Everyone had moments where they imagined hurting someone, Christ, Janine had entertained a few scenarios herself, but to this extent?

The car, a new model Ford, had been put out by the fire brigade, and she'd been given clearance to come closer. Despite being in protectives, she was still careful not to walk on anything but the evidence steps—there was so much blood spatter it brought on nausea. The road was peppered with it.

From what she could gather, the driver's-side window had been broken from the outside—at first, she'd thought it had shattered from the pressure of the fire, but looking at it now, all that blackened glass on the seat, not on the road, it told the correct story.

What was going on here? Was this linked to the Bracknell murders? The pathologist would say not, the MO wasn't the same. Then again, the bloke in the alley had been strangled, and the woman in the car had her throat slit. *This* fella...fucking hell, the blunt force trauma was overkill. Someone seriously arsey had committed this murder.

"Nasty," Radburn said beside her. "An anger killing if ever there was one."

"Hmm." Janine studied the body. "We can't even see his face. Whatever was used has obliterated it. This feels a bit personal, don't you think?"

"Or we're dealing with a nutter who enjoys going over the top for the sake of it."

I know only one man who does that. "Yep."

So why hadn't George phoned her if he'd done it? Could this be nothing to do with him? Was it Mule? Had one of his drug sales gone wrong—again? Come to think of it, George's time was up there. In the morning, Janine would mention a tip-off from a Bracknell resident who didn't want to be named. She'd then set the ball rolling in making a show of finding Mule. They'd hit a dead end with the Bracknell murders, so hauling him in would reap some results.

Come on, George. If this is you, get a shift on and ring me.

Her burner bleated. *Talk of the devil…*

"Excuse me while I take this," she said.

"Personal calls on work time. I don't know…" Radburn smiled.

It bugged her. Who was he to make a comment like that? "I told you, I have a sister who has issues and I can't not answer when she gets in contact. She sometimes falls over, and we both know how long it takes for an ambulance to come these days. If she needs help, I can get there quicker." Janine didn't have a sister. Using one as an excuse for George or Greg ringing her had come in handy since Radburn had been assigned to her team. Her DS was a by-the-book type, and she couldn't risk him getting suspicious.

She navigated the evidence steps and walked over towards a car tyre place, out of the way of people who'd hear her side of the conversation. People like Radburn who'd find it interesting and maybe report her for being a bent copper. She took the phone out and swiped the screen.

"Are you calling to tell me about the body on the industrial estate?" she whispered. Part of her wanted George or Greg to say no. It would mean she wouldn't have to tread lightly and worry herself silly about steering the case in another direction.

"Yeah. Ford on fire, bloke battered to death. It was me," George said.

Shit. This was unlike George—well, the setting, the area. He didn't usually do anything so out in the open. "What the fuck for?"

"He was raping one of Debbie's girls."

"Jesus. And how did you just happen to be here?"

"She phoned me. We have a new system. I told you about it. You're the one who vets the fucking punters for us."

A job she hated doing. Running all those names through the database without a valid reason could trip her up, especially when they weren't related to any of the cases she was working on. PNC searches revealed unspent convictions, cautions, warnings, or reprimands on someone's record, and she mainly looked for issues with abuse, sexual assault, and outright rapes so she could warn the twins not to allow any of Debbie's girls to engage with those men. To appease her seniors, she'd made out one of her contacts asked for the searches to be done as she was watching the backs of sex workers. The woman in question, a social worker, didn't exist, but Janine's ruse had held up so far. She worried that one day her house of cards would come tumbling down, though, and she'd be exposed for the dodgy officer she was.

"So what's this dead fella's name then? One of the men already on the 'okay' list?" she asked, although she'd know soon enough. The check on his number plate was currently being dealt with by someone at the station.

"No idea. The girl forgot to go through the proper channels with him."

What a stupid woman, ignoring safeguards laid down to keep her safe. "There's a lesson there. I bet she won't be dismissing your rules in future."

"Hmm. Can you cover this up?"

She glanced around. Already, the weight of this crap pushed down her shoulders. She loved working for The Brothers, earning extra money, getting a thrill from straddling both camps, but sometimes it got too much. "There's the hurdle of CCTV I have to jump over, you know that, right?"

"Already sorted with our fella. The two cameras that would have picked me up doing the deed, he deals with them."

"So you didn't have to go through your council bloke, then."

"No, those ones are private."

She imagined some of her team trawling through the feed and seeing nothing but an empty road, which wouldn't make a lick of sense and would prove the feed had been doctored. They'd be looking for a murder in action, and not seeing one would raise a humungous red flag. "What is your man doing with the cameras?"

"Deleting the murder and making it look like the cameras went down just beforehand."

That was one worry off her back. "Which vehicle did you use?"

"The taxi."

"That's something, then. There's so many of them around here, it could be anyone. I have to say, though, this is a bit of a fuck-up."

"I know. But it was an emergency."

"Think things through next time. Like phoning me when one of the girls is being attacked. Easier to deal with."

"I lost the plot."

She sighed. "Tell me something new. Thanks for landing this one in my lap."

"Sarky cow."

"You're lucky I was called out. It could have been someone else."

"Silver linings and all that. Every cloud's got one."

She wanted to bawl him out, but George and Greg had warned her about getting ideas above her station before, so she refrained and acted the good girl. "I'm going forward on Mule in the morning. Just warning you."

"Right."

"Have you dealt with him yet?"

"Nope, first thing."

"Are you letting him go afterwards?"

"No."

"For fuck's sake, George!" she hissed. "I need him for the Bracknell murders."

"Think about it. How will you explain the state he'll be in if I drop him off somewhere, beaten up? That will lead to more investigating, and if he dies from his injuries, you'll have to find a killer's killer. A headache for you. All that paperwork. I'll tell you what, I'll get him to write a confession. I'll post it to the station."

"That's better than nothing, I suppose."

"It's all you're going to get."

He cut her off, and she stared at the phone, fucked off beyond reason.

That bloody bloke. Christ Almighty.

She returned to Radburn who cocked his head and narrowed his eyes at her. Fuck, he looked like he'd been thinking things she didn't want him to think. Why couldn't she have chosen her own DS? She prided herself in being able to read people well, and she'd have picked someone who wasn't that interested in their job and wouldn't give a shit what she was doing.

"That was a long conversation," he said. "Is your sister okay?"

"She had a panic attack, and I had to talk her down from the ledge."

"What's up with her?"

The lies tripped off her tongue. "Anxiety, depression, you name it."

"How can you be expected to take so many calls for her while you're working? She does know that if she distracts you from a crime scene, you could make mistakes, doesn't she?"

Not with you here, Mr Beady Eyes. You'll have great satisfaction in telling me if I've missed something. "Depressed people tend to only focus on themselves, which is natural. It's fine. I can handle it."

"What, by getting her to see a counsellor or something?"

"That's not a bad shout," she said to appease him, all the while thinking: *Then I'll have to think of another excuse as to why I'm answering a personal phone at work. Or ask for you to be moved to another team, but I can't exactly state my reason as you being bloody nosy.* That was a headache she didn't need. There would be questions, and the DCI would likely refuse her request anyway.

311

Yes, sometimes, this extra job she had with the twins was definitely too much.

Chapter Twenty-Three

Apart from what The Brothers had told him, Mule didn't really have a clue why he was here. Why it was a warehouse and not, say, a forest, so they could kick the shit out of him and string him up from a tree. Wasn't that what happened on the telly? Sitting on this chair all night, tied to it with rope, this was hardcore stuff. These two weren't fucking about. He'd pissed himself a couple of times, unable to hold it, and he was barely keeping a shit inside. The two men who babysat him, Will and Martin (he'd listened to them talking to each other, using their names), had been pleasant enough, although Will had given Mule a few hard glares from time to time, especially when he'd had to mop up the piss.

Mule had spoken to the man on the rack. Norton, claiming to be a private investigator, had said he'd been employed to find some lad who'd run away. He didn't see why he should be here when he'd only been doing his job. The fact he'd used a gun, on The Cardigan Estate of all places, seemed to have gone over his head.

Mule supposed a few things had gone over *his* head, too. He should have asked for permission to sell drugs, but instead, he'd grown ballsy and reckoned he could duck and dive, keeping out of the twins' way. His attitude had caught up with him, and here he was, staring at George and Greg who stood in front of him, their faces expressing exactly what they thought of him.

Scum, that's what he was to them.

As for the unknown fella they'd brought in, who appeared dead but had twitched a few times overnight, who was *he*? Going by the conversation between one of the twins and Will, the fella, Steve, had been run over. His legs were at odd angles, and one of his shoes was missing. A large gash on his forehead churned Mule's stomach. Was that from hitting the windscreen or the ground? Either way, it was gross, and with the three of them here, it just went to show how mad the twins were. Mule had heard the rumours, but he'd stupidly thought they'd been inflated, like folklore or Chinese whispers that added bullshit with every new generation.

"So, tell us about the murders," Greg said. "Why did you kill that bloke and woman? Dean and Laura."

Mule jolted from the shock of that statement. "I didn't kill anyone!"

"So you say," Greg said.

"I'm telling you, I've got fuck all to do with it. Someone else was there, at the end of the alley."

"Convenient," Greg muttered. "How many people bring out that old chestnut? Believe me, loads of them do. You had all night in here to think about it, and *that's* all you could come up with as your story? Someone else did it? Bollocks. George had a call, and a woman told him you were the killer, you must have been seen. What have you got to say about that?"

"They're lying. This bloke, he came along in a taxi and —"

"A *taxi*?" Greg said and looked at his brother, eyebrows low.

George shrugged.

"Yeah, a black cab," Mule said. "I thought the bloke I was selling to had arranged for it to pick him up. Dean, you said, yeah? I don't know anything about a woman. It was just me and the buyer until Mr Taxi came along."

"George?" Greg said.

"Don't look at *me*. I was with Janet."

"You'd better have been," Greg mumbled.

What was going on here then? Mule had heard they were always together, so who was this Janet? Why had mention of a taxi got Greg eyeing his twin up like that? Was one twin accusing the other of murder?

George glared at Mule. "So let's go with your fantasy theory for now. I'll indulge you for a minute or two. Mr Taxi arrived. What happened then?"

"He came storming over just as I was making the sale, and I legged it. I hadn't seen him before, and in my line of work, when strangers are about, it either means my cover's been blown and I'm about to get carted off down the nick, or someone's pissed off I'm selling and they want me to stop. Like, they want to take over my patch. Have you even heard of that lot from Birmingham? There's a gang of them, bigger pickings than me. It's them you need to catch."

"Birmingham?" George asked.

"Yeah, they're a nasty lot of fuckers. The main one's name is Fletcher, and he's hard as fuck. You want to watch out for him."

"Where is he based in London?"

"I don't know. All I *do* know is he plans to sell all over the city."

"We'll be poking into that. What did Mr Taxi look like?"

"He had a beard. And I *watched* him do the kill. I stood in the dark when he thought I'd gone and saw it all. He *strangled* the buyer against the wall. Bloody well held him up until he died. Once I realised what was going on, I legged it."

"Where did you go?"

"Home."

"What was it about Mr Taxi that had you scarpering? Have you got some sort of gauge you go by where if they look a certain way, you're off?"

"He was big, and I mean big, like you. Something was off about him."

"Did you worry it was someone to do with us?" George sneered. "Did you crap your little pants that you'd been dealing without permission and we could have found out about it?"

"Something like that."

George walked behind Mule, out of sight. Mule had seen what was on that table when he'd been brought in, and he reckoned George was going to hurt him with one of those tools. A presence at his back and Greg staring that way had Mule nearly letting go of his bowels. A fumbling at his side relaxed him somewhat. George was undoing the rope. Was that it? Was he allowed to go now?

"Get up," George said. "I want you to do me a favour."

Mule stood, his legs so stiff from being in the same position for hours. George beckoned him over the table, and Mule almost refused to follow. Why would he willingly move towards those tools? Why would he encourage the big man to use them on him?

"See this pad?" George prodded it with a gloved finger. "You're going to write a nice letter saying you killed those people. You're going to use their names—Dean and Laura, remember. You'll say you had a fight with the fella and the woman witnessed you strangling him, so you had to get rid of her an' all."

"Why?" Greg asked, coming to stand beside George. "Janine can get a confession out of Mule. Let the police handle him."

Mule's bowels complained. "Fucking hell, what? I didn't *do* anything!"

"This'll save her a load of hassle," George said.

Greg shook his head and walked away. "I don't know what goes on in your brain sometimes. This bastard has killed. Yes, he's done us wrong, but it would be more of a lesson to let him serve his time. To allow him to live until he's released, and *then* we'll come for him. The torture of worrying about the day he gets his freedom is sweet justice in my book. It doesn't always have to end in death straight away."

"You've changed your tune. What was it that happened recently? Remember me wanting to

319

give a certain cretin a second chance because he bleated on about his mum? What happened there? It went wrong, *that's* what happened. We end this clown now and be done with it."

"Fine."

George smiled at Mule. "Here's a pen. Get writing."

"Then you're going to kill me?" Mule knew the answer; panic had forced him to ask the question. The only reason he'd write a confession was in the hope they'd murder him quickly. If he refused, he'd endure torture, and he couldn't handle it.

"Weren't you taking a blind bit of notice of our conversation just then? Of *course* I'm going to fucking kill you. Unlike my brother here, I want immediate justice for *us*. I don't care whether our copper could do with the kudos of taking you down and getting you put in the nick. You wronged us. You went behind our backs. *That's* why I'll kill you."

Greg came back over. "Why didn't you just say that to me in the first place, then? Fucking hell!"

"I'd have thought you'd realise," George said. "Because it's what we *do*."

Mule picked up the pen. This was insane, admitting to something he hadn't done, but what choice did he have? He couldn't run, couldn't escape, and he'd die no matter what he said or did. He wrote a confession, tears falling, and oddly, he thought of the state of his house, what with him leaving that bath running. Not only would his mother have to grieve her son, she'd have the hassle of dealing with the insurance company.

"My mum," he said, finishing the last line. "The coppers will take her flat, the one I bought her. Seize it because it was bought with illegal proceeds."

"We'll let our copper know to leave your mum out of it," George said. "We're not monsters."

You could have fooled me.

"Go and sit down," George barked.

Mule walked over to the chair, thinking it would be the last time he was ever on his feet. He thought of his life before he'd gone into dealing drugs. His ex-girlfriend who'd left him because he'd got up to no good. His sister who'd once looked up to him and now didn't speak. And his mum. Oh God, his poor mum.

The shot to his forehead put an end to all that.

"What the fuck's up with you?" Greg stared at George, incredulous. "You *shot* him? Is that *it*?"

What the hell was going on with his brother? He'd been acting differently for a day or so, and this bollocks just worried Greg even more. George rarely just shot someone. He liked to torture, to do as many nasty things as his warped mind could conjure up.

George smiled, a weird smile that bothered Greg. It was as if he was *pleased* with himself for only shooting the bloke.

"Sometimes," George said, "the simple route proves things."

"Proves things?" Greg frowned.

"Yeah."

"Do you want to explain that?"

"Nah." George walked off towards their captive on the rack. "Help me get this twat down, will you?"

Greg stared at his twin's back. Something was *well* off.

Norton was bricking it, as you do when you're yanked off a rack, your back sore from the spikes digging into your skin through your clothes all night, then plonked on a chair that someone had just been shot in. Seeing the back of a head explode and knowing you'd be next was right up there as being one of *the* most terrifying things that could happen to you. All because he'd wanted to make some money so his wife would shut up about him not earning enough. To make matters worse, she wouldn't even take any notice that he was missing. She'd assume he was on a stakeout. It wasn't unheard of for him to not come home for days on end. He'd told her not to phone him while he was on the big jobs, he needed to concentrate, and she'd accepted that without complaint.

Now, he wished she was the sort to touch base every so often. Then again, if she had an emergency, she would expect his phone to be off, so her not getting a reply wouldn't be an issue either, it wouldn't make her think something was wrong.

She wasn't a lifeline, wasn't anyone who could help him, and neither were any of the men here.

The dead lad, Mule, had told him his life story in raspy whispers during the night. How he'd been brought up poor, and the only way he'd found to make easy money was selling drugs. Lots of them. He owned a semi-detached gaff— and had complained that it had probably flooded by now, on account of a bath being left running, something he was riled up about in the extreme— plus he'd paid for his mum's flat. He had nice things, good food, and now it was all gone. Just like that, everything he'd worked for had disappeared.

The same was about to happen to Norton. He wasn't stupid. He only wished he'd told Steve to fuck off and do one when he'd approached him about finding Albie. Too late to have recriminations now, though. The Brothers had caught up with him, and the fact he'd shot their friend was enough for them to shoot *him*. Albie aside, and that stupid Sarah bitch, he was a goner.

Steve had muttered at one point when Mule had dropped off to sleep. He'd asked Norton where he was, why his bed was so hard, and Norton had assumed Steve was delirious, especially when he'd screamed at an attempt to move. Being run over must be fucking painful,

Norton got that, but what he didn't get was, why had the twins bothered bringing him here to finish him off? Why not roll over him a couple more times in the car and kill him there and then?

"Why did you find it necessary to shoot our friend?" George asked.

I knew that was what bugged them the most. "He could have identified me."

"Your daft number plate did that. Considering what you do for a living—or should I say *did*—you'd think you'd have switched it out for something else like you did with your car. Yes, we know you have another vehicle. So what's the van for?"

"Stakeouts, so I can sleep in the back or whatever."

"And abduction," George said, toying with the gun he held.

"Well, yeah, I needed to put Albie somewhere he wouldn't be seen."

"And what were you meant to do with Albie once you'd taken him to that flat?"

"I was to drop him off, get paid the last of my money by Steve, then go home."

"Lucky for us, you went to the pub. Saved us having to let your wife know why we were carting you away. Can you imagine, us turning up at your house? All the neighbours seeing? The missus crying?"

"What does it matter? You marched me out of the pub in front of everyone anyway. Someone's going to report that."

"D'you think so? That's where you're wrong. We had a natter with the landlord before we approached you, and he knows what to do. He'd have told everyone in that pub to keep their mouths shut or The Brothers would have something to say about it. The pub's on our manor, the landlord's under our protection. No one will give a shiny shite what happens to you. How much did Steve owe you?"

"A grand."

"Then we'll see that your wife gets it." George paced and slapped the gun against his palm. "Now then, I'd usually hurt you. I'd have thought up something hideous to do to you, involving a tool, and you'd be screaming, begging to die. Today is different. Today I'm showing myself I can do this without having to resort to extreme violence. We all know what you've done, and I don't feel it's necessary for us to go through it all from the beginning, do you? It's boring. It's a waste of our time. So if there's any message you'd like us to deliver to anyone, now's the moment to say it. I've got an itchy trigger finger, and looking at your ugly mug is giving me the willies."

What could Norton say? That he was sorry? That he hadn't meant for it to go as far as it had? That he wished he'd never set eyes on Steve? What was the point in pleading his case? He wasn't going to live no matter what he said.

"I've got nothing to say."

The end.

"Have you been having sessions with Janet the past two nights and lied to me, saying you're on dates?" Greg asked.

"No, why?"

"Two quick deaths. It isn't like you."

"I'm trying something new." George turned and shot Steve in the head.

"What the fuck did you do that for? Why didn't you ask him where Aster's mother is? The body?"

"If you were more observant, you'd have seen he died about two minutes ago."

Greg ran a hand down his face, thankful his brother had gone down the shooting route but surprised regardless—and annoyed at himself that he hadn't noticed Steve had already carked it. Will and Martin stared as if George had grown a second head. There was more to this than met the eye. If his twin was suppressing Mad George, why? Had Janet finally got through to him? Greg couldn't imagine George never indulging in torture again, it wasn't him, it wasn't normal.

When Mule had mentioned a taxi turning up, Greg had suspected George straight away. His first feelings had been those of hurt, of being left out of the loop, George wanting to go it alone. Then he'd tossed that aside, because there was no way George would keep anything from him.

"Do you want to do a rampage again?" Greg asked, "like recently? A few Cheshires and kneecappings? If you're suppressing your need for violence in here, you'll be needing to get it out somewhere else."

"No," George said. "I'm all right. Everything will be fine."

"You told Norton you were doing this to prove a point to yourself. Well, you've proved it, well done, but I'm worried if you keep Mad tucked up for too long, you'll do yourself some damage."

"I don't need Mad anymore."

"I don't believe you. What was it you said? You were lost without him, you weren't yourself. I've already noticed a change, and it isn't sitting right."

"Thought you didn't like me going off on one the way I do."

"I don't."

"Shut up then." George did that smile again.

Greg had a well uneasy feeling, and he didn't like it. "Are you going to tell me next that you don't want to saw these fuckers up?"

"Nah, I still don't mind doing that." George wandered into the bathroom and came out carrying a forensic suit. "If I can get these done inside an hour, we can go to the Taj for a slap-up lunch." He glanced over a Martin and Will. "You two can get off now. Martin, before you fall into bed, take some of the petty cash from your place and visit Zoe Callaghan—I'll message you her address. Give her a hundred quid for leccy and the usual for an ear's wages, and make that amount one of your weekly stops."

"Will do."

The men left, and Greg put slices of bodies in black bags as George cut them up. He'd get to the bottom of this weird behaviour in the end.

"Seeing Janet tonight?" Greg asked between cuts.

"Nah, she's off to Wales for a conference. Won't be back until Monday."

Good.

Chapter Twenty-Four

Spring had sprung upon the UK, the day gorgeous, the sun shining through Jane's freshly cleaned windows. She had finally moved into her new flat, got away from her abusive ex-husband who now languished at His Majesty's pleasure. She'd never have to see him again, and her move to London from Jersey, plus her name change, meant she could relax and live the life she'd dreamt of before she'd met him.

If it wasn't for the horrendous smell coming from somewhere, everything would be perfect. It had been fainter when she'd first come to view the flat, but yesterday, moving day, it had been stronger. The removal men hadn't seemed bothered when she'd mentioned it, going on about blocked drains and how Jane would have to look into who dealt with that sort of thing. In some blocks of flats, the residents had to share the costs of things like that. She was renting, so it didn't bother her. The landlord would foot any bills.

She went out onto the landing, sure it emanated from the place next door, which had apparently been empty for a while, according to the man who lived at the far end of the landing. A gaggle of flies marched on the floor in front of the door, sluggish and bloated, some taking flight and heading straight for her. She batted them away and moved closer, sniffing.

Something was definitely going on in there.

Heart going like the clappers, she dialled nine-nine-nine.

"The stench is always the worst in cases like this," Janine said to Radburn, trying not to laugh at his expression. "It gets right up the nostrils and lives there for a bit. Once, I smelled it for *days* afterwards."

"It fucking stinks. I'm going out for some air."

Had she found his Achille's heel? She'd wondered if he had one. Up until now, he'd been professional, well put together, nothing ruffling him. It seemed the odour of a decomposed body was one thing he couldn't handle. Granted, it wasn't pleasant, a mix between rotting meat and that nasty juice that accumulated at the bottom of a too-full kitchen bin, now stale because the corpse had been there for so long, but for some reason, she'd thought nothing would affect him.

It pleased her that he wasn't Mr Perfect.

Janine stared at the remains on a leather sofa. She didn't need the pathologist to tell her how long it had been here. Going by the Nikes and the bracelet, items described to the police as something Colin Weston owned, this was the fella who'd been shot upstairs a few weeks ago. At the time of officers attending the scene, the body had been missing, although it had been clear the man had been murdered there. All of the residents had been spoken to, according to reports, but it was obvious whoever lived here hadn't said a word. The uniforms who'd been on duty doing house-to-house had some explaining to do. One of them anyway. They'd hidden the fact that this flat had either been overlooked or mention of getting no answer at the door hadn't been logged.

She'd have to poke into who owned the flat and where they were. Or was this linked to the kerfuffle involving Aster, the girl the twins had helped out? George hadn't mentioned that a body was inside the flat, so maybe he hadn't known. If he had, why hadn't he said anything to her?

She sighed and left the flat, taking her protectives off and putting them in the designated bag. She nodded to SOCO who milled around on the landing, although she suspected any clues would be long gone by now. Apparently, a cleaner mopped all the landings, stairs, and the foyer on a weekly basis. Still, they had to try.

She went down the stairs to the ground floor and, instead of going out the front where

Radburn was possibly trying to stop himself from being sick, she opted for the back, a communal garden with benches, a fountain, and grass newly mown. Checking she was alone, she phoned the twins.

"Know anything about a body?" She gave them the address.

"Err, it'll be tied to Aster's saga."

"I suspected as much. And you didn't think to tell me?"

"We didn't know there was a body. Last Aster knew, he'd been shot by her father when he'd tried to help her. What happened after that, she had no clue."

"And where is her father now?"

"Guess."

"Oh, for fuck's sake. Do you know who owns the flat?"

"Um, some woman who's now dead. Aster's father killed her years ago. Karen someone or other."

"Do you know what he did with her body?"

"No idea."

"Does Aster?"

"Leave her alone. She's just settling into a life knowing she's safe."

"Fine."

She sat on a bench and stuffed the burner away, asking herself if she could cope with this shit for much longer. Now she understood why Clarke, her predecessor, had reckoned it was a good idea to create a plot to kill The Brothers. He'd probably thought it was his only way out of messes like these. The pressure working for the twins was higher than she'd anticipated. She swore she had a stomach ulcer.

Janine would just have to plod on. And be more careful. Radburn was a lovely bloke, but he still questioned her a lot. Especially about her 'sister' and why she had to take her calls, even though she'd explained all that. He was mainly concerned as to why Janine had to keep stepping away to speak to her privately when she'd said she'd consider getting her a counsellor.

Much as she liked him, he may become a problem.

One for the twins to sort? Maybe.

Ida smiled smugly. She sat on a chair in the dining area of her kitchen and held her feet up.

"Nice shoes, these, although it's been a while since you bought them for me."

George smiled and slid his phone away. He seemed annoyed about something. They'd refused to explain what Steve had been up to, which pissed her off. She'd asked them to come back and tell her, but so far, they'd avoided the subject.

"Need anything else?" George asked.

"I wouldn't say no to a matching handbag for when I go down the market on a Saturday."

George handed her two fifty-pound notes. "You're getting expensive, young lady."

Young? No one had called her that for years.

She poured tea. "I witnessed a murder and warned all the neighbours who saw you run Steve over to keep their mouths shut, so this is my wages. There's more stuff I've got my eye on, so you won't be getting rid of me yet." She smiled wide. "Fancy a rock cake?"

Chapter Twenty-Five

For people who loved their fathers, knowing he was dead would usually bring on floods of tears and a long stay in Mourning Crescent. Aster felt nothing but relief, happiness surging through her that she was free of him, free of his crimes, free from being punished for her part in them. The house would stand empty—she didn't want it. It had been a shock to find out the old woman neighbour was complicit in him being knocked down and her husband had once worked for Ron Cardigan. It just went to show, you shouldn't judge a book by its cover.

Aster wandered around the flat she rented off the twins. It was much bigger than the other one, and she had a terrace all to herself, seeing as she was on the top floor. She'd planted some flowers in ceramic pots and dotted them about, and the two deckchairs had been a bargain at twenty quid for the pair. They were both occupied, one by Aster, the other by Kallie, who'd come round once again to ponder where Sarah had got to.

"It's just so weird that she'd ghost me like that for all this time," Kallie said. "I mean, I thought we were *friends*."

Aster shrugged. She couldn't tell Kallie that after Sarah had been shot and sewn up, Moon had dealt with her. It had seemed daft for her to have gone to the clinic and been tended to if the twins were only going to give the order for her to die anyway, but there had been so much going on at that time, maybe they hadn't been thinking straight.

Did Aster feel bad that Sarah was dead? At first, yes, until George had let her know that she'd confessed to Moon that she hadn't given a shit what would happen to Aster, she'd just wanted the money Norton had offered. Aster had long since learnt that the twins didn't play by the usual rules, and their logic was simple: if you pissed someone off who they cared about, if you hurt them, they were sorted.

"Some people are like that," Aster said. "Friends only when it suits them. I did ask The Brothers to put feelers out, and they said Sarah had got a job offer abroad."

"See, that's so odd. Why didn't she just say? She never even told her mum."

Aster's stomach rolled over. "You went round to see her, then?"

"Obviously. She's reported her as missing, but the police don't seem to be doing anything about it. Like the twins, they discovered she's gone off to work in Italy or something. They're not even bothered about finding her to make sure she's really there. Janine Sheldon or something, that's the copper's name who was dealing with it."

Aster marvelled at how things worked on Cardigan, how the machine was so well-oiled, shit just got swept under many rugs. "Well, Sarah's obviously changed her phone number and everything and wants a fresh start. Maybe she had stuff going on that you didn't know about. Secrets or something."

"I don't buy it. Something's off."

While Kallie rattled on, going over and over the same old ground, Aster half listened while thinking of how her fortunes had changed. She now worked for the twins, well, for Janet, as a secretary. Janet had given Aster a few sessions, and she'd worked wonders in showing her she wasn't to blame for her father's behaviour. Aster had confessed to killing Muttley, and it had been good to get it off her chest.

"Sometimes, we're forced to do things we'd rather not," Janet had said. "It's up to us to see if our consciences will allow us to move on."

Great advice, and Aster had discovered her conscience was fine, thank you. She was free to be herself now, no looking over her shoulder, no one calling her nasty names. She owed her freedom to the twins and would do anything they asked of her now.

Aster sighed. Kallie was prattling on about phoning the police in Italy to see if they could find out whether Sarah was there. Aster was going to have to phone George and Greg when Kallie had gone.

Her 'friend' was becoming a bit of a problem.

Chapter Twenty-Six

Zoe Callaghan had a yearning for all things nice. When her ex had left, she'd been thrown back into poverty, something she'd known all too well as a child. She didn't want her own kids going through the same thing, hence her working on Debbie's corner for a short while. Life had taken a turn when an angel had come in the form of a ginger George Wilkes who'd taken away her need to spread her legs just to keep warm. To begin with, she'd been their ears in the sense that if she heard any gossip they needed to know about, she passed it on. Since then, she'd been elevated, sent out on what she privately referred to as detective missions, the pay much more than her job at a clothes shop called The Boutique, so she'd left there to concentrate on the twins' matters.

She currently sat in a coffee shop, monitoring her target, Macey Moorhouse. Macey was thirty-five, no kids, no husband, and had a penchant for shoplifting. Zoe had known her from when she'd been caught thieving in The Boutique, and the woman had blipped The Brothers' radar because she'd stolen an expensive item from an emporium they'd recently acquired. Not even the manager knew George and Greg owned it. They'd renamed it Vintage Finds, and it sold high-end clothing, shoes, and all manner of things people could want when it came to dolling themselves up in the trends of years gone by.

Macey had nicked a necklace worth two grand.

Zoe leant closer to listen to Macey's phone call, feigning reaching for her purse in her bag.

"I want a grand for it. What do you mean, is it even real? Of *course* it fucking is. How do I know? Dur, isn't it obvious? I had it valued, didn't I. You'd be getting it at half the price." A pause. "I'm in Bumble's Café. Yeah, I'll wait for you, but no longer than an hour, all right, and bring cash."

Excitement ploughed through Zoe. She was about to see the sale go down in front of her once the buyer turned up. She took her phone out of her bag and opened her camera app, ready to snap pictures. God, she was a right old Miss Marple.

Twenty minutes passed, Macey watching out of the window, Zoe watching her.

Macey's phone rang. "Why am I selling it so cheap? It's *hot*, that's why. I need to get shot of it quick." She drummed her long, shocking-pink nails on the tabletop. "How hot? Err, think the surface of the sun, mate. What do you *mean* you don't want it, then? Fuck's sake. Whatever." She jabbed at her screen and looked Zoe's way. "What are you fucking staring at?"

"I'm not staring. Blimey, keep your hair on."

"Mind your business. Didn't anyone ever tell you that listening to things that don't concern you only leads to trouble?"

347

It led to trouble all right, but Zoe wasn't the one in the shit.

Zoe smirked.

"What's so funny?" Macey demanded.

"Nothing."

"Good. Keep it that way."

Macey got up and trounced out of the café. Zoe waited for one minute then followed. It was exciting, doing what she did, and she thanked God for the day George had rescued her.

Ahead, a commotion drew her attention. A cluster of people had gathered on the pavement, and a blue sports car zoomed off up the road. Zoe quickened her pace, elbowing into the crowd. Macey was on the ground, a hand to a bleeding gash on her forehead.

"He took my bag," she said. "Shit a brick, he took my effing bag…"

Zoe dashed out into the road to get the number plate, but the car had gone. Of course it bloody had, it had driven off at high speed. Had the person on the other end of the call sent someone round here to nick the necklace? They must have done.

She returned to Macey.

A man had helped her up, and she slapped at his hands that held her steady.

"I'm not a fucking old biddy. Get your filthy paws off me, pervert."

The man stepped away, alarmed. "Suit yourself." He strode off, glancing back and frowning.

Macey dusted herself down and stared at the smear of blood left on one hand. The rest she'd wiped on her white blouse. "Fucking great. Not only has he robbed my bag, but I'll have to pay for this to be dry-cleaned now."

The blouse retailed at sixty-five pounds; it was one of many Macey had lifted from The Boutique when Zoe had worked there.

Zoe walked away, phone to her ear. It rang twice, then George answered. "The necklace has been nicked off Macey. Someone snatched her bag. Blue sports car with a big spoiler on the back and a red sticker of some sort on the bumper."

"Shit, I know who that is."

"Are they a problem?"

"Yeah, you could say that. Cheers."

Zoe popped her phone away and walked towards home. She just had enough time to put her feet up for an hour or so before she picked the kids up from school. Tomorrow, she reckoned she'd get the call to lure Macey to the twins.

That gobby cow had no idea what was coming her way.

To be continued in *Refugee*, The Cardigan Estate 17

Printed in Great Britain
by Amazon

18360472R00205